A Tin Star for Braddock

Other Avalon Books by James A. Janke

MCHENRY'S LAST SHOOT-OUT

A TIN STAR FOR BRADDOCK

JAMES A. JANKE

AVALON BOOKS
THOMAS BOUREGY AND COMPANY, INC.
401 LAFAYETTE STREET
NEW YORK, NEW YORK 10003

PRINTED IN THE UNITED STATES OF AMERICA
ON ACID-FREE PAPER
BY HADDON CRAFTSMEN, SCRANTON, PENNSYLVANIA

Dedicated to
Laura and Andrew

Chapter One

Clay Braddock licked at the trickle of sweat that reached his mouth. The sweat was salty, and the dirt on his face mixed with it to make a paste that dried his lips even more.

He glanced around at the buildings on either side of the dusty street as his horse plodded wearily down its center in the baking, midafternoon sun. "Not much of a town, Nick," he said. But his horse paid him no attention. "Green Valley," he went on. "Humph. Fancy name for a place that looks like it could just dry up and blow away one of these days. And about the only green thing we've seen for miles is cactus."

Braddock turned his mount toward a horse trough in front of the Desert Hole saloon. The horse caught a whiff of the scent of water and stretched his neck out. Braddock smiled. "Yeah, me too."

The horse reached the trough and stuck its muzzle down deep inside. Instantly, Braddock heard the slurping of the thirsty animal.

He dismounted gratefully and stretched himself to his full six feet. Then he arched his back and stretched his arms out to the side and twisted them. "Feels good to be on my own feet again, Nick,'' he said and patted the horse on the neck. ''We've come a long way, ol' boy.'' The horse shifted on its feet, still lapping up the water noisily.

Braddock peered into the trough. There was not much water in it, but he was surprised that there was any at all. He thought that the saloon owner would have given up on keeping water in the trough in this kind of heat. The water looked stale and warm—but very wet.

He smiled, unbuckled his gun belt, and removed it. After buckling it again, he hooked it over the pommel of his saddle. Then he took off his hat and plopped it on top of the gun belt. Next he unbuttoned his shirt and pulled the tails out. But he left his leather vest on.

''Move over, Nick,'' he said. He stepped closer to the trough, reached down, and scooped up the water. He splashed it onto his face and poked dripping fingers into his ears. He rubbed the water into his eyes, then cupped his hands and poured handfuls over his head. He splashed water onto his chest and wiped off the sweat and grime of the hot, dusty miles.

Suddenly, a shrill cry from the boardwalk caught his attention, and he turned and saw a young woman trying to twist herself from the grasp of a large man who blocked her way. Very pretty, she was wearing a yellow and white dress that contrasted sharply with the black hair that bounced at her neck from under her bonnet. And the dress showed off her slender form, even if it did have a ballooning skirt. Her face was fine-featured, with a pleasing complexion that showed she didn't spend every day indoors.

The man, on the other hand, was ugly. He was tall and heavy, and although fairly young, he had a definite potbelly that wasn't covered by his leather vest flapping in the breeze. He had a bulbous nose and fat jowls, and wore baggy pants stuffed sloppily into his boots. A holster hung low on his right hip.

"Let go of me!" the young woman demanded. She slapped at the wrist holding her arm.

"Aw, nursey," the man said, "I just need a little tendin' to."

"You're not sick!" she snapped at him.

"Well, how 'bout a little dance then?" He tried to pull her closer.

Another man, the big man's companion, was laughing. "Told you she was a wild filly, Milo," he said.

Her assailant laughed when the woman smacked his hat down over his eyes. "Oh, want to play in the dark, huh?" He grabbed both her arms now. "I like games in the dark. Come here, pretty Sally."

"Miss Anderson to you!" she growled. She kicked him in the leg as hard as her awkward position would allow, but Milo didn't even flinch.

Braddock quickly wiped the excess water from his face and ran his hands over his hair as he stepped to the saddle. He buttoned his shirt as fast as he could and tucked it in.

The woman let out a sharp cry again. "Stop it! Stop it!" Milo and his companion laughed in response.

Braddock quickly put his hat on and slung his gun belt over his left shoulder. He grabbed Nick's reins and moved the reluctant animal the few steps to the hitching rail. Then he strode toward the boardwalk in front of the saloon, holding the holster against his chest with his left hand.

Both men on the boardwalk were laughing, Milo with his hat still pushed down over his face. The woman was struggling to back up. They were now directly in front of the saloon door.

Braddock mounted the two steps to the boardwalk and deliberately bumped into the struggling pair. "Oh, excuse me," he said. "You're blocking my way."

The woman stopped struggling and looked at him in surprise. Milo said "Huh?" and he let go of the woman with one hand and fumbled for his hat with the other so that he could see. He pushed the hat up and looked at Braddock.

"I said," Braddock repeated calmly, "you're blocking the door."

Milo put his free hand on his hip and scowled at Braddock. "Then go around," he said. He still held on to the woman's arm with the other hand. "I'm busy here."

"Well, be busy somewhere else. This is a public boardwalk and you're in my way."

Milo looked back at his companion in astonishment. "Can you believe this guy, Wes?" he asked.

The other man shrugged. "Guess he doesn't know who you are."

The woman jerked free of her big captor and jumped off the boardwalk.

"Hey!" Milo said, and he started after her. Braddock quickly sidestepped and blocked his way.

The young woman paused and looked up at Braddock. "Thank you, sir," she said, and then she strode quickly away.

Milo put both hands on his hips and glared at Braddock. Tall as Braddock was, Milo still had a good three inches on him.

"Now you really spoiled my fun with that nursey, mister." Milo started to circle Braddock, sizing him up. "I think I'll have some fun with you instead."

"Sorry," Braddock said. "I'm thirsty." And he quickly stepped to the batwing doors of the saloon.

"Hey!" Milo started after him as he entered the saloon. The batwing doors swung back and forth on their hinges.

"Forget him for now," Wes said. "We gotta see McIntyre, remember?"

Milo stopped. "I didn't forget." He watched Braddock walk deeper into the saloon. "But I ain't done him with him yet. Later."

"Sure. Plenty of time."

Milo stalked off down the boardwalk, and his shorter companion had to hurry to catch up.

Inside the saloon Braddock approached the bar and glanced around. He was surprised at the number of men in the saloon.

"What'll you have, mister?" the glum bartender said as he flipped a dirty towel over his shoulder.

Braddock nodded at him. "Howdy." He tipped his hat back on his head a bit, and he didn't bother to take the gun belt from his shoulder. "Your sign outside says the beer's cold. Is it?"

"Nope," the bartender said. "All the ice melted months ago."

"Hmm. Well, I'll have a beer, anyway."

"Okay." The bartender left him and then came back with a foaming mug.

Braddock picked up the mug and raised it toward his lips.

The bartender held out a cupped hand. "We expect payment before you drink, mister. One dollar."

Braddock let the mug sink slowly. "Okay, but a dollar's an awful lot for a beer. A warm beer at that."

"Doesn't seem to make any difference to our other customers. And I don't suppose you're any better than they are."

Braddock was surprised at the bartender's attitude, but he fished into his back pocket, pulled out a silver dollar, and slapped it down. "I could have bought ten beers for this where I come from." He raised the mug to his lips and started a long drink.

"Well, you ain't where you come from." The bartender slipped the dollar off the counter. "You're here, and we gotta get our money in advance. Can't tell if you got a job or not or whether you can get one."

Braddock lowered the mug with a smile. "Ahh.

Warm or not, it's still wet." He set the mug on the bar top and then jerked a thumb over his shoulder. "That why there are so many fellows here on a Thursday afternoon? No jobs?"

"Those that got hired don't seem to have much to do yet," the bartender said. "And those that didn't get hired don't have anything to do, anyway. Which man you come here to work for—Davis or McIntyre?"

"I'm not here to work for either one."

"The others will be glad to hear that. Lot more men already here than can get hired."

Braddock took another drink. "Well, I'm just passing through. On my way north to Montana to my sister's. Her husband died a while ago, and I'm going up there to help her and her three kids run the ranch."

"Cowhand, huh?"

"Yup. Been a cowhand and horse wrangler half my life, since I was fourteen. Not much to show for all of it, though. Just what I got on Nick outside."

"Nick?"

"My horse. So this may turn out to be as close to a place of my own as I'll ever get. My sister's got a little spread along the Yellowstone."

"Then you've got a mighty long ride ahead of you."

"Been traveling a week already," Braddock said, remembering the endless miles in the saddle. "Figure I'm maybe two-thirds of the way. Who are Davis and McIntyre?"

"What do you care? You don't want to work for either of 'em."

"You know, you're not the friendliest bartender I've ever met. Back where I come from—"

The bartender shrugged. "Why don't you go back there?" He turned his back and started to walk away. "Let me know if you want another beer."

"Not at a dollar apiece. Hey, you got any food?"

The bartender stopped and looked back. "Beans and bread. Want some?"

"How much?"

"A dollar."

Braddock grunted in disgust. "Figures. All I can eat?"

"Each plate."

Braddock sighed. "That figures too. Okay, I'll take a plateful."

The bartender went through a door behind the bar and returned in a minute carrying a tin plate with a thin covering of beans and a chunk of bread. He plunked down the plate in front of Braddock. "One dollar. In advance."

Braddock already had another silver dollar out of his back pocket. "Figured that ahead of time," he said, and plinked the coin down on the bar top. He looked down at the skimpy portion of food. "Somehow the generous helping doesn't surprise me, either,"

"Let me guess," the bartender said. "Back where you come from—"

"That's right. And back where I come from, I'd get a fork or a spoon. Or do I have to pay for them too?"

"No charge." The bartender reached under the bar,

brought up a big spoon, and plopped it into the beans. Some sauce spattered onto Braddock's shirt.

Braddock brushed at the sauce. "Think I'll sit at a table." He glared at the bartender. "Where the company's better." He picked up the beer mug and plate.

The bartender shrugged.

Braddock walked over to the nearest table and set the plate and mug down. He placed the gun belt on the table, pulled out a chair, and then sat down. He started to eat, scooping up the beans in big mouthfuls. They were cold and not thoroughly cooked. But they were delicious.

He tried to eat them slowly, remembering how much they had cost him, but it didn't take him long to clean up the plate. He scraped all the sauce up with the spoon and would have licked the plate too, but he didn't want to do that in public.

He leaned back in the chair and picked up the beer mug for a long drink. Then he settled back, rested his elbows on the arms of the chair, and idly crossed his fingers. He glanced at the other men in the saloon. There were almost a dozen, at a time when he would have expected the bartender to be just about alone. Several men wore suits or striped white shirts with shoestring ties and no coat, but their clothes looked a bit threadbare. The other men wore clothes like his own, those of a man who worked outdoors. But their clothes didn't look dirty, just rumpled. The men seemed to be having a good time. Braddock noticed that every man wore a gun belt, which meant they were probably gunfighters.

He didn't like gunfighters, and he figured that most cowhands didn't like them. Even in a drought there was work to be done on a ranch, and gunfighters weren't workers. They didn't produce anything. They just sat around and drank and ate up supplies and lived off other people's greed, hate, or tragedy. They were just plain trouble.

"There he is, Milo," a man from outside the saloon said.

Braddock jerked his head toward the entrance. He saw Milo looking straight at him over the batwing doors.

"I see him," Milo said. He punched the doors with his fists and strode in. The doors banged up against the inside wall.

Braddock clenched his teeth and tensed. This time the big man had three other men with him, not just one as before. And Braddock now realized that Milo and his men were gunfighters too, which meant big trouble for him.

Milo strode up to the table Braddock was sitting at. He stopped, planted his feet apart, and put his fists on his hips. "Get up!" he ordered. The man called Wes stopped next to Milo, and the other two men stood a few steps behind him. All conversation in the saloon stopped.

Braddock looked up at Milo. "I'm not done with my beer yet," he said. He glanced at the other three men. They were smiling, but the smiles weren't friendly.

Milo reached down and clamped both hands on Braddock's vest. He heaved him to his feet, knocking the chair over backward. Braddock came up easily; he didn't want his vest ripped.

"We got some unfinished business before you leave," the big man said. "If you ever do leave." His companions snickered.

"What unfinished business?"

Milo twisted Braddock's vest and pulled him closer. "You took my fun away from me earlier."

"I'm sorry," Braddock said evenly, "but you were blocking the door. I merely asked you politely to move aside."

"I'm used to people going around me."

"And I'm used to people being polite," Braddock informed him. "You're wrinkling my vest. Please let go."

Milo smirked. "And if I don't?"

"I'll have to make you," Braddock said matter-of-factly.

The three men with Milo burst into laughter.

Milo glanced down at Braddock's gun belt on the table. "That's mighty big talk for a man who ain't even wearin' any iron."

"A man doesn't need a gun to handle a little boy," Braddock said, and he was pleased to see Milo's jaw tighten, his eyes bulge, his head quiver, and his control wane. Braddock preferred to fight men who weren't thinking too clearly.

Milo suddenly let go of Braddock's vest and took a short step back. "You stopped the little nursey from havin' a dance with me before, big talker. Now let's see if you can dance yourself." He went for his gun, and he was quick. The pistol seemed to spring into his right hand of its own will. He had the pistol cocked before the gun was out of the holster.

But Braddock was fast too. His left hand shot straight out, and by the time Milo had his gun leveled, he had jammed his forefinger between the hammer and the firing pin, and his hand had clamped down firmly on the gun.

"Go ahead," Braddock said simply. "Shoot."

Milo looked down at the useless weapon in his hand. Boisterous laughter broke out in the crowd in the saloon. Milo's companions glared at the laughers. But it had no effect.

Braddock spoke again: "Where I come from, it's not polite to draw a gun on a man."

More laughter.

Milo bared his teeth, and a growl rose in his throat. His body tightened, getting ready to attack.

Braddock drove his right fist straight up and into Milo's clenched jaw. The hand went sailing on up as Milo's head snapped back. Braddock could picture Milo's brain sloshing up against the front of his skull.

As Milo's eyes turned upward, he slowly tipped backward and then crashed to the floor like a giant tree felled in a forest. The spittoon on the floor at the end of the bar bounced at the impact, and every crack between the floorboards sent up a little puff of dust.

Braddock was left holding Milo's pistol in his left hand, his finger still planted beneath the hammer.

Wes, next to Milo, went for his own gun. Braddock snapped the gun around, grabbed it with his right hand, pulled the trigger, and flicked the hammer back with his left forefinger. The hammer slammed down on the firing pin, the gun fired, and a slug smashed into the gunman's upper arm.

Wes screamed, dropped his gun, and spiraled down to the floor. He clamped his other hand on the gaping wound in his arm and writhed and screamed.

Braddock had cocked the gun with his right thumb and was pointing it at the next man. That man got his pistol halfway out of his holster, but he froze when he saw the muzzle pointed at him.

Braddock scowled. "Draw it or drop it!" he snapped.

The only correct response was obvious. The man let go. The gun plopped back into its holster.

Braddock gave the third man still standing a fierce look, but that man still had his thumbs hooked in his belt. His mouth was agape, but he quickly blurted, "No play here, mister. Honest."

Braddock glanced about the room. He hadn't expected trouble from that quarter and none seemed imminent. He looked down at Milo. The man was lying flat on his back, his arms limp at his sides. His head had squashed his hat, his mouth was open, and his eyes were closed. He was breathing evenly.

Braddock called over his shoulder to the bartender without looking in that direction: "You got a doctor in this town?"

"Yeah," the bartender said. "Those fellows know where his office is. The doc's been pretty busy these days."

Braddock steadied the pistol on the two men who were standing. They were staring at him, waiting nervously. "Drop your gun belts, slowly," he ordered.

They nodded. "Yes, sir." They unbuckled their belts and let them drop to the floor.

"Now pick up your wounded friend there and take him over to the doctor."

They nodded again. "Yes, sir." They bent down quickly to help Wes, still rolling on the floor in pain. They struggled to get him to his feet. He screamed in pain again.

"I'll leave your guns here with the bartender," Braddock said. "You can pick them up later."

They nodded quickly. "Yes, sir. Okay." The wounded man stopped screaming and now started to whimper in anguish. "It's busted," he cried. "It's busted!"

"We'll get you to the doc, Wes," one of the gunmen said. "Let's go." They headed slowly for the door.

Braddock let the hammer down on his gun. Then he picked up the wounded man's gun from the floor and tossed both pistols on the table. Finally he picked up the two gun belts and their weapons.

Chairs scraped in the saloon. Men rose. They started toward Braddock. He edged toward the table as he looked at the crowd approaching him. "He drew first," he said. He dropped the gun belts on the table, but his right hand stayed near a pistol handle. His eyes darted warily from one man to the next.

A man in front nodded vigorously. "Absolutely. It was a fair fight. No question about it. We all saw it."

There was a murmur of agreement from the other men.

The man in the lead came up to Braddock and offered a handshake. "My name's Hanson. Tyler Hanson." He smiled warmly.

Hanson was one of the men wearing a suit. It was dark blue with a buttoned vest to match, and dust showed conspicuously against the dark color. The suit looked awfully hot today, but it did give the man a certain look of authority. So did the gun belt and pistol he wore under his suit coat. The leather glistened and the buckle was bright and shiny.

Braddock shook the hand cautiously. "Clay Braddock."

Hanson jerked a thumb over his shoulder. "These are two of my boys—Jim Wells and Dave Reever." The two gunmen nodded toward Braddock.

Braddock nodded back. He noticed that Hanson's two subordinates were not dressed as nattily. But there was no mistaking the importance they assigned to their pistols.

Hanson placed a boot on the seat of a chair at the table and rested his arm on his knee. "That was a mighty fine piece of action, Braddock."

"Maybe," Braddock said. He reached for his gun belt and put it on.

"Going up against four armed men without even wearing a gun," Hanson said. "That took guts."

"I do a lot of dumb things."

"I don't see it that way. You didn't even hesitate. That combination of guts and skill can be very profitable around here nowadays."

"Oh? This have anything to do with these fellows named Davis and McIntyre?"

Hanson nodded. "It does. We work for Davis." He nodded at the rest of the men in the saloon. "Some of these other men do too. And some of them work for McIntyre." He poked a finger towards Milo, still lying unconscious on the floor. "My friend there works for McIntyre too."

"Is that a fact?" Braddock stuck the two loose pistols in his belt and looped the two remaining gun belts over his arm. Then he picked up the mug and drained the last of the beer. He picked up the plate too, and headed for the bar.

Hanson followed Braddock, as did his two men. The rest of the crowd went back to their tables. "Look, Davis gave me the authority to hire any man I felt I could use. And he pays good money."

Braddock set the mug and plate down on the counter. He slapped down the two gun belts too, and the two loose pistols from his belt. "Keep these for a while," he said to the bartender.

The bartender nodded casually and stuck all the pistols and gun belts under the counter.

Braddock looked at Hanson. "To do what?"

Hanson shrugged. "Whatever needs doing."

"That's what I thought." Braddock hoped his disgust didn't show too much. He nodded down at Milo. "Is he really your friend? How come you work on opposite sides?"

"Yes, he's really a friend of mine. We just got hired by different sides, that's all. It's our work. Friendship can't interfere with that." Hanson stepped next to Braddock and leaned on the bar. "Can I buy you another beer?"

Braddock shook his head. He looked down at Milo. "He won't be out much longer, and I'm not interested in still being here when he comes to. He won't be fooled so easily the next time."

"You're right about that," Hanson said. "And Wes Carter isn't going to be too happy about having his arm shot up, either. Those two friends of his, Billy Stickle and Elmo Flick, might take exception to your actions too." Hanson nodded down at Milo. "But Milo's a mighty proud man. Whatever the other three might do, you're either going to have kill Milo or leave town."

"You're pretty casual about your friend's fate. But don't worry. I'll leave town."

"Not so fast." Hanson placed a hand on Braddock's shoulder to slow him down.

Braddock stiffened.

Hanson let go promptly. "Look, there are these two big ranches in this valley. And some little ones too. But they don't count for nothing. Anyway, these two big ranchers, Davis and McIntyre, are at each other's throats. The valley's not big enough for both of 'em. With this drought they've had for a couple of years now, the range just can't support so many ranches. And to top it all off, Davis's boy Earl was killed about a month ago, and McIntyre's son Douglas is being blamed for it. The law can't do anything about it, so Davis means to have it out with McIntyre himself."

Braddock nodded down at Milo. "And McIntyre feels the same way about Davis, right?"

"Sure. McIntyre swears his boy didn't do it, but he's as eager to get rid of Davis as Davis is to get rid of him. So one way or the other, one of them will have to go."

"And you think Davis is the one in the right?"

Hanson laughed. "There isn't any right or wrong to this. Davis just made me a better offer, that's all."

"I see. The richest one wins, huh?"

"The *strongest* one," Hanson said.

"Or the luckiest," Braddock countered.

Hanson laughed again. "You may be right about that."

"This is going to be a disaster. A lot of men are going to get killed."

Hanson slapped Braddock on the shoulder. "Hey, that's what some of us are getting paid for. We take their money and take our chances. It's part of our work."

"Not mine."

"Davis could use you. He'll pay you more than you make in a year as a cowhand."

"But I'll probably be alive a year from now as a cowhand." Braddock started for the door. "So long."

Hanson followed him. "McIntyre will probably try to hire you. Even after what you did to Milo here. I'd rather have you working on my side."

"No, thanks," Braddock said. "By nightfall I want to be far away from here."

The bartender leaned on the bar. "No need to be in such a big hurry to leave, mister."

Braddock stopped and looked at the bartender. "I don't like the way this town treats women and strangers. I don't like this town. And," he added with emphasis, leaning a little closer, "I don't like you."

The bartender shrugged. "Well, those three men you sent to the doc feel the same way toward you."

"I'll do them a favor too and leave town," Braddock said. He started for the door again.

"They made sure you wouldn't leave."

"What?" Braddock asked. "How?" He reached the door and paused to squint at the bright sunlight outside.

"They stole your horse," the bartender said.

Chapter Two

Braddock clapped his hands on the top of the batwing doors and stuck his head outside. Nick was definitely gone.

He spun his head around. "Why didn't you say something?" he asked angrily. He stormed over to the bar and slammed his fist down on the counter. He glared at the bartender. "Where I come from we hang horse thieves."

The bartender shrugged. "Not my fight. You're the one who got 'em mad at you. You watch your own horse."

Hanson stepped up next to Braddock. "Ah, that's a tough break," he said.

Braddock glanced at the gunfighter briefly. Then he stalked to the doorway and flung the doors open angrily. He strode out onto the boardwalk, stopped, and planted both fists on his hips. He clenched his teeth as he looked both ways. Not much moved on the street, and there was no sign of Nick.

Hanson joined him. "Don't suppose you got another horse, huh?"

" 'Course not!" Braddock snapped. He squinted

down the long, dusty street. "Is that a marshal's office I see? I need the law."

"That's the marshal's office, all right," Hanson said. "But he's not there. He's over at the other end of the street." He nodded in that direction.

Braddock looked that way, but he saw no lawman. "I don't see any marshal."

"In the cemetery."

Braddock looked quickly at Hanson. "What?" His hands dropped to his side.

"Two days ago. Died sudden-like."

"I don't suppose he died naturally."

"Well," Hanson drawled, "with eight to ten bullets in him, Marshal Tate just kind of naturally dropped dead." He grinned a little.

Braddock didn't say anything at first. These gunfighters! Hanson thought the marshal's being murdered was funny. "You have anything to do with that?" he asked.

"No. Wasn't any of Davis's men, in fact. Nor McIntyre's, for that matter."

"Well, then, who did it?"

"Some of the gunnies in town with nothing to do but get drunk and make a lot of noise. Tate tried to quiet 'em down. Mistake."

"I guess so," Braddock said. "Did the marshal have any deputies?"

"One. He headed for Denver within half an hour after the marshal died."

"Sounds like a good idea on the deputy's part."

"But now you have no one to help you," Hanson pointed out.

Braddock hooked his thumbs in his gun belt. He nodded slowly and sighed.

"Now, if you were working for Davis," Hanson said, "some of the boys and I could help you get your horse back. They were McIntyre's men, so that makes you an enemy of his. And an enemy of McIntyre's is a friend of Davis's, I'd say."

Braddock shook his head slowly. "I'm no one's enemy. Leave me out of this war."

"You're on your own then." Hanson shrugged. "Can't help you."

"I'll handle it. Where's that doctor's office? They must have gone there."

Hanson pointed. "Turn right at that general store. Doc Anderson's office is at the end of the street on the left side."

"Thanks," Braddock said, and he started in that direction.

"If you change your mind," Hanson called after him, "I'll still be here."

"No, thanks."

Braddock reached the end of the boardwalk and stepped off it onto the dusty street. He strode briskly, his boots kicking up dust. His brow furrowed, he reached into his back pocket and fished out his remaining coins. Two dollars and ten cents. Enough for one more meal and a beer. "Wish I'd kept riding," he muttered to himself. He thought about the rest of his money in his saddlebags. There was little enough of it, but right now it seemed like a lot. But it was Nick and his saddle and gear and the other things in his saddlebags that he wanted back the most.

He shoved the coins back into his pants pocket as he turned the corner. The street facing him was short, and it was a quick walk to Doc Anderson's office. A small white sign with black lettering above the side door of a neat white clapboard house identified the office. Braddock stepped onto the low boardwalk and went up to the door. He was about to knock when he read the small sign that said to step right in. He opened the door.

Sally Anderson yelped a little on the other side. She had been about to open the door herself. "You startled me," she said. Then she recognized Braddock at the same time he recognized her.

"You!" they both said.

Braddock chuckled, but Sally's look was serious.

He glanced at her attire. She was wearing a large apron that covered her from her neck to the hem of her dress, which was light blue with a straight skirt. Her short sleeves were rolled up even higher, and there was blood on the apron. She was holding a gunnysack in one hand.

"Now I remember that Milo called you a nurse," Braddock said.

"Yes. I help my father."

"Are you now helping your father with that wounded

man, Wes, who was just brought over here by his two friends?''

''Yes,'' she said, and lifted the sack slightly. There was a large dark stain in one corner. ''This is his arm.''

Braddock flinched. ''You cut his arm off?''

''Your bullet shattered the bone beyond repair.''

''He drew on me first. I could have put the bullet through his heart and no one would have called me on it.''

She nodded slightly, then said, ''Thank you again for helping me out of an awkward situation with that Milo fellow.''

''You're welcome. Where I come from, women are treated with respect.''

''What can we do for you? Are you hurt too?''

''I'm looking for Wes's two friends—Billy and Elmo. They stole my horse.''

''I'm sorry to hear that. They're not here, and they didn't leave a horse. They rode off as soon as they dropped off the wounded man.''

''Sally,'' a voice called from the interior.

''We're not done with the gunfighter yet,'' Sally told Braddock. ''We still have to close the wound. Since you're here, could you be of some help so I can get back to help my father?'' She held up the sack. ''Please take care of this. Walk about two hundred yards into the desert and bury it.''

''I don't have time for that,'' he complained. ''I've got to get after those two men and my horse.''

''You don't even know where to look for your

horse." Then Sally smiled. It was a little smile, but a small dimple appeared in each cheek, and Braddock was sure there was a twinkle in her brown eyes. "Please?" she said.

Braddock hesitated. Every minute meant that Nick was getting farther away. But Nick's brown eyes had never had the effect on him that Sally's eyes were having. He reached for the sack and said, "Is there a shovel somewhere?"

"In the shed in back," she said. "Thank you."

About twenty minutes later, in the desert, he set the grisly sack down and started to dig. Finally, after a half hour, he was able to pat the dirt flat on the little mound he'd created. Catching his breath after his exertion under the hot sun, he rested on the handle of the shovel while he observed a few moments of silence for the part of a man he had buried.

He walked back to the shed and put away the shovel. He thought about going after Nick immediately, but he returned to the doctor's office instead. He admitted to himself that it was just for the chance of having another conversation with Sally Anderson.

He entered the office without knocking. The room was small, with a desk and a few chairs. A row of thick books lined the rear of the desktop. Several wall shelves were stocked with bottles and little boxes. On one wall hung a chart of a human skeleton.

Through a door, Braddock could see a wooden operating table with straps hanging down. There was a pile of bloody bandages on the center of the table, and a lot of surgical instruments on a small, high table next to it.

Sally entered the operating room from a side room Braddock couldn't see and scooped up the bandages. She saw Braddock standing in the office. "All finished?" she asked.

"Yes. How's the patient?"

"Do you really care?" Her voice was not critical, just curious.

"Yes, I really care. I know how I'd feel if I'd had my own arm cut off."

She tossed the bandages onto a bench in the corner and then entered the office. "Maybe you do care. But you don't seem too concerned about your horse."

"I'm very concerned about my horse," Braddock countered. "Not only my horse, but all my gear and personal belongings are on him. All I've got left is what you see in front of you."

Sally frowned sympathetically. "They work for Angus McIntyre. That's all I can tell you."

Dr. Anderson entered. He was not much taller than his daughter, with a slim build. His shirtsleeves were rolled up and he, too, was wearing an apron. He was wiping his hands on a cloth. "You the man they call Braddock?"

"Yes, sir."

The doctor flung the cloth over his shoulder. "Well, your patient is still under the anesthetic, but he'll be around shortly."

"Then what?"

"That's a good question," Anderson sat down in the chair at his desk. "Medically, he'll have to stay here for a while until he recovers from the shock of surgery. But you have to realize that this Wes fellow is now a gunfighter without a right arm. You took his living away from him."

"He tried to kill me," Braddock declared. "Should I feel sorry for him?"

"No. You had cause for what you did. But you can be sure that McIntyre feels no responsibility for the man. His friends might care, but what are they going to do for him?"

"What's your point?"

"I think Father is telling you that the man will be awfully angry when he's able to get up, regardless of the rightness of your actions."

Braddock took off his hat and wiped the sweat from his brow. "Yes, I figured that. But as soon as I get my horse back, I'll clear out of here. This is no place to be with a war about to erupt."

Anderson nodded vigorously. "You're wise, Mr. Braddock. This town, this whole valley has gone crazy."

"The drought shouldn't turn the ranchers on each other," Braddock said. "They can't blame each other for the weather. The rain will return eventually. For the time being, they should just work together to survive."

Anderson folded his arms casually and leaned back. "It goes back a lot further than that. Davis and Mc-

Intyre have been at odds since they both came to this valley almost thirty years ago. They're both bull-headed, and the valley wasn't big enough for the two of them back then, and now it truly isn't big enough for any two big ranches. This is the third straight summer of severe drought. It's devastating all the ranchers."

"It was the murder of Earl Davis about a month ago that really inflamed the situation," Sally said.

"Yes," her father agreed. "Earl was Davis's oldest boy, his pride and joy."

"Did McIntyre do it?"

"Lester Richards, who's the town mayor and a banker, saw it happen," Anderson said. "Says it was McIntyre's son, Douglas."

"I heard that the law didn't do anything about it."

Anderson shook his head. "Oh, Marshal Tate investigated, all right, but McIntyre swore it couldn't have been Doug. Says he's got a dozen witnesses who'll say Doug was elsewhere at the time. And, of course, he's got a lot of guns that say it wasn't Doug too. Marshal Tate was just one man."

"Davis is out for blood now," Sally said. "Both ranchers are hiring gunfighters, and there's been fighting already."

Anderson jerked a thumb toward the inner room. "That wasn't the first arm I've amputated in the last month. And I've removed lead and patched up bullet holes and knife wounds and busted noses."

"And four other men have died since Earl's death," Sally added.

Anderson pulled open a drawer and brought out a bottle of liquor and two glasses. "I always take a drink after surgery," he told Braddock. "Never before. You want one?"

"No, thanks. Got to keep my wits about me too."

"Were you using your wits when you went up against four gunmen without a gun?" Sally asked.

"Wes's friends told you?"

"No, but the news traveled fast. You're quite a celebrity already." She was smiling now.

"Humph. I'm a cowhand, not a gunfighter. What good would one pistol have done me against four professionals? I knew there was going to be a fight, but I figured I had a better chance of staying alive if I didn't use a gun."

Anderson laughed. "That's the most sense I've seen anyone around here show for a long time." He had poured himself a drink, and he tossed it back. "Ahh." He set the glass down. "Good stuff," he said. He looked up at Braddock. "You also show good sense by getting out of town as fast as you can. I've half a mind to do so myself."

"You know you won't leave these people when they need you," Sally said. "You've been in this valley almost as long as Davis and McIntyre."

Anderson grunted toward his daughter. "Bringing it on themselves, daughter. So far, it's been just gunfighters and drifters who have gotten hurt—except for the marshal." He looked at Braddock. "A good man, the marshal."

Braddock nodded. "He made a mistake, I was told."

"He was doing his duty," Anderson said. He turned the glass in his hand. "But his duty was made impossible because the town's just stoking the fires. They shouldn't be encouraging all these bored men with nothing to do to come to town and hang around looking for excitement. It's bound to create trouble here in town, no matter what Davis and McIntyre do to each other. The town doesn't seem to care as long as they keep spending money." Anderson shook his head. "Money isn't that important."

"Well, my money is pretty important to me," Braddock said. "And I really need to get my horse."

"Wish we could be of some help," Sally said.

"You have been. Thank you."

Anderson frowned. "For what? We didn't do anything for you."

"You convinced me that I'm right about getting out of town as fast as I can."

Anderson smiled and nodded. "Sensible. More sense than all the young men who've ever called on you, daughter."

"Father," Sally said sternly. She glared at him.

Braddock smiled. "Well, they showed a lot of sense by coming to call, Dr. Anderson."

Anderson smiled also, and he took Sally's hand affectionately. "I'll agree with you there."

Sally, embarrassed, slipped out of his grasp. "Father."

"Miss Anderson, it's been a pleasure to meet you," Braddock said with a slight bow.

"Nice to have met you, Mr. Braddock. I hope you find your horse."

"So do I." Braddock put on his hat and said goodbye.

The doctor waved a hand. "Good luck, sir," he replied.

Braddock left and closed the door behind him. He started walking back down the street he had come. He sighed deeply with a double problem. Sally Anderson really took his breath away, but he would probably never see her again, and that thought pained him. But how was he going to get Nick back?

"Mr. Braddock?" someone called from the door of the general store at the corner. The man beckoned to the inside of the store, and two other men emerged. One of the men was quickly trying to get a suit coat on. The other two already had theirs on.

Braddock stopped and watched the three men approach hastily across the dusty street. He checked immediately to see if they were wearing guns. They weren't.

As the three men joined him on the boardwalk, the one in front shook his hand enthusiastically. "Pleased to meet you, Mr. Braddock," he said. "I'm Lester Richards."

Braddock recalled that this was the man who had seen the murder.

Richards introduced the other two men: "This is Mike Bennett, owner of the Golden Riches saloon, and this is Mortimer Taylor, owner of the general store."

"Gentlemen." Braddock shook each of their eager hands. He was puzzled by the reception.

"Mr. Richards is the banker in town," Taylor said.

"So I've heard."

"I also have some interest in a few stores," Richards said. "And the Desert Hole, and a few other ventures, some ranching, et cetera."

"Uh-huh."

"We heard about your performance with McIntyre's men, Mr. Braddock," Bennett told him. "Mighty fine, sir, mighty fine."

"Yes, well, I really need to be going, gentlemen." Braddock started edging away.

Richards grabbed him by the arm. But he quickly let go when Braddock squinted at him. "Sorry," he said, and brushed at the sleeve. "We are just so eager to talk to you."

"Why?"

"Well, we three men constitute the town council," Richards said. "In fact, I'm the mayor."

"I know that too. What does that have to do with me?"

Richards laughed politely. "Well, sir, we are offering you the job of town marshal!"

Chapter Three

Braddock's mouth dropped open. "Marshal?" he sputtered. "Did you forget what happened to your last marshal?" He started to stomp away.

"Wait, wait!" Richards caught up to him. "You haven't heard our offer."

"Whatever it is, it isn't worth dying for."

"Marshal Tate was a little too zealous in the performance of his duties," Richards said. "You don't have to be so extreme."

Bennett joined in: "Those boys were just having a little fun in my saloon, Mr. Braddock. I don't mind a few bullet holes here and there."

Braddock looked at him. "As long as they spend plenty in your place. Is that right?"

"Well, frankly, yes," Bennett admitted.

"All these men are spending a lot of money in town," Taylor said. "Davis and McIntyre have each hired almost an army, and they're paying top dollar."

"What are the gunfighters doing in town?" Braddock asked. "Why don't Davis and McIntyre keep them out on their ranches? It's just asking for trouble for both sides to be mixing like that, with nothing to do.''

Richards waved his hands. ''This won't last long. To be quite frank with you, both Davis and McIntyre are running into cash problems. My bank has lent them a lot of money lately, but we've reached the limit on how much we can lend them. The ranches in the valley are no longer the best collateral, you know. This drought, the dreadful markets for cattle, the—''

''Wait a minute.'' Braddock held up a hand. ''You mean you've been lending these two ranchers money to hire gunfighters?''

''That's right,'' Richards said. ''It's not my business what they do with the money.''

''And then the gunfighters spend it in town, so the saloon owners and merchants get the money, and they deposit it in the bank. Then the bank lends the money to Davis and McIntyre again, and it just goes round and round, the ranchers going deeper and deeper in debt, and the town getting richer and richer.''

Richards stroked his chin. ''Well. . . .''

''Forget it,'' Braddock said. He waved them off and started walking again.

All three men caught up to him and kept pace.

Richards went on: ''Green Valley will pay you a hundred dollars a month, Mr. Braddock. That's well above what a town marshal usually gets.''

Braddock raised his eyebrows at the generous salary, but it didn't persuade him in the least. He shook his head. ''I'm no gunfighter,'' he explained as he kept walking. "Almost every one of the men hired by those two ranchers could probably beat me in a draw, if it came to that. And they're all looking for trouble. Gunfighters mean nothing but trouble. You just haven't learned that yet."

"We're not asking you to take on the gunfighters, to stop the range war," Bennett said. "Your job will simply be to protect the citizens and property of this town. Within reason. Let the men have their fun, and don't get in the middle of their fights. They're hired for that. It's not your job to stop them."

"When bullets fly, they don't care who they hit," Braddock said.

Taylor tried now. "You can lodge in the marshal's office and the town will pay for all your ammunition and all your food. The doctor's daughter will cook your meals."

Braddock stopped short. The other men surged ahead and had to come back. "Sally Anderson?" Braddock asked. "She cooks for the marshal?"

"Green Valley pays the Andersons to provide food and medical care for the jail's prisoners and the marshal. We're a small town. We need a doctor, but there isn't much business for a doctor, so this little side job helps them make do."

Braddock considered that. Sally Anderson cooking his meals? "Does the marshal eat at the Andersons'?"

"If there are no prisoners in the jail. Otherwise, she brings the food to the marshal and his prisoners."

Bennett stepped closer and smiled. "Right pretty young woman, that Sally Anderson."

Taylor added: "There isn't a young man in the valley who wouldn't like to have dinner at Sally Anderson's table, Mr. Braddock. All the Davis boys and Doug McIntyre, too, tried to—"

Braddock shook his head firmly. "No. There just wouldn't be too many meals before I'd be dead." He started walking again.

"Mr. Braddock," Taylor begged.

Braddock stopped. "Gentlemen, please. The answer is no. I'm going to rent myself a horse at the livery stable, go find Billy Stickle and Elmo Flick, get Nick back, and then head for Montana. Good day." He turned and walked on.

The three other men stopped, and Taylor said, "Josh Miller might not rent you a horse."

"Money will get anything in this town," Braddock replied. But he had to admit to himself that he wasn't sure what two dollars and ten cents would buy.

The three townsmen watched him go. "Stubborn man," Richards commented.

"But not stupid," Bennett said.

Braddock found Miller's livery on the main street at the far west end of town. The two big doors in front were open. A man inside was sweeping dirty straw out the front entrance and raising a cloud of dust in the process.

Braddock walked inside. " 'Afternoon," he said. "Mr. Miller?"

The man stopped sweeping and looked up. "That's me, stranger. What can I do for you?"

Braddock was surprised at how old the man was. He was about six inches shorter than Braddock, but obviously weighed a good deal more. He didn't look fit enough to be sweeping, much less running a livery stable.

"I want to rent a horse for a day," he said. "Do you have any?"

"Sure. I got a couple." He gave Braddock a look up and down. "You look like a cowhand, mister."

"I am."

"Where's your own horse?"

"Stolen. I want to go after the men who took him."

Miller's eyebrows rose. "Custer's mustard, mister. How do I know they won't shoot you and keep my horse too?"

"I won't give them the chance, believe me."

Miller squinted at Braddock. "Are you that fellow who took on the four gunmen in the Desert Hole?"

Braddock sighed. "Yes."

"H'm. Well, maybe you will get the drop on 'em. Tell you what. Ten dollars. I'll rent you a horse for ten dollars."

Braddock's fists went to his hips. "Ten dollars? Where I come from, it wouldn't cost me more than a single dollar for just one day."

"I'm takin' a risk, mister," Miller said.

Braddock let his hands down. "All right, ten dollars. I don't have the time to argue with you. But I'll have to pay you when I find my horse. I don't have ten dollars on me, but I got more than that on my horse.''

Miller set the broom aside and came up close to Braddock. Braddock could smell a heavy mixture of liquor and tobacco on Miller's breath. ''And what makes you think the men who stole your horse haven't already spent your money?''

''Well, what other choice do I have?'' Braddock roared.

''I don't know, but I'm not rentin' you a horse until I see the ten dollars. So there.'' Miller stared at Braddock.

''Never mind,'' Braddock said finally. He turned and strode out of the barn.

Richards was leaning on the open door. ''Green Valley also provides its marshal with a horse, Mr. Braddock,'' he said with a smile.

Braddock shook his head. ''Still no deal, Mr. Richards.'' He kept walking down the dusty street, but he had no idea of a destination.

''Braddock!'' a man off to the side shouted.

Braddock turned his head. Milo was standing in the middle of the side street with his left hand hooked over the buckle of his gun belt and his right hand dangling at his side, near the handle of his pistol.

''Milo, isn't it?'' Braddock said. His heart started to race. He was sure he was no match for Milo in a draw.

''I got a score to settle with you.'' Milo started rubbing the fingers of his right hand together.

''With a gun?'' Braddock asked. ''Don't you think

you can take me with your fists? Does your head still hurt too much?''

Milo's fingers stopped.

Without looking away from Milo, Braddock pointed with his left hand toward Richards, still standing in front of the livery stable. Josh Miller had come out to watch too. ''What are those men going to tell everybody? I'm not going to draw on you.''

Milo looked past Braddock.

''You just can't shoot him down,'' Miller said.

''No?'' Milo bellowed.

Braddock started to unbuckle his gun belt. ''Let's have at it.'' He dropped his gun belt to the ground. Then he tried to spit into his two hands. But his mouth had gone dry. He rubbed his hands together and started to shuffle about. He brought his fists up. ''Come on, big man. Come on.''

''Now he isn't even wearing a gun,'' Miller said.

Milo eyed Richards and Miller. He looked back at Braddock. ''All right,'' he said, trying to sound enthusiastic. ''I'll enjoy it more this way, anyway.'' He unbuckled his gun belt and let it slide to the ground. He balled up his fists and started toward Braddock. ''How many pieces should I bust you up into?''

Braddock and Milo started shuffling about in a circle. Milo swung first. Braddock easily dodged. He landed a punch into Milo's stomach, but the big man did not even seem to notice. And then a lightning stroke of a punch flashed out and caught Braddock on the jaw.

Braddock stumbled backward. Milo was a powerful

man, and he lunged at Braddock and hammered several more punches to his head. Braddock blunted the blows with his forearms, but they still hurt. He managed only a couple of glancing blows himself.

Milo charged with his head down. Braddock smashed him on the side of his head just as Milo drove into his stomach. The air whooshed out of Braddock's lungs, and he staggered back. Milo kept pushing and finally Braddock toppled over.

But Braddock grabbed Milo's belt as he went down and heaved the big man over him as he hit the ground. The maneuver did not work well because of Milo's weight, and Milo wound up on top of Braddock, though face-up. Braddock beat on Milo's face, and Milo rolled off and over and leaped to his feet. Braddock was amazed at the speed of the big man. His pear shape belied an agility that matched Braddock's.

Braddock tried to get to his feet too, but Milo was over him again, and then a massive fist smashed down on his cheek and ripped a gash open. Braddock collapsed flat on the ground, and he shuddered at the pain in his cheek and the feel of warm blood gushing down his neck.

Milo laughed. He raised a boot and brought it down toward Braddock's head. Braddock slipped aside. He grabbed the boot when it hit the ground and rolled into it. Milo was knocked over.

Braddock struggled to his feet. A quick touch of his cheek brought a grimace and another shudder. There was a large flap of skin hanging from his cheek. His palm came away covered with blood.

Milo got to his feet. He was smiling. "Maybe you'll just bleed to death right there," he said. He started forward again, hunkering down, hands extended, fingers wriggling like claws. "I'll just rip your skin clean off your body."

Braddock backed up, his fists ready. "Come on, you big buffalo, you ugly overstuffed cow, you fat, repulsive pig."

Milo yelled and charged, head down. He plowed into Braddock, but Braddock managed to turn sideways just as Milo hit him. Braddock couldn't stop Milo's huge bulk from driving him backward, but he caught Milo's head under his arm instead of in his stomach.

Braddock scampered back, trying as hard as he could not to fall over again. To his surprise, they collided with the side of the livery stable, and Milo's head smashed right through a board.

Braddock bounced off the wall and fell down to his hands and knees. He rose quickly to his feet and spun around to defend himself. But Milo wasn't moving. He lay limply on the ground with his head resting inside the building on the broken board that he had knocked clean off the wall.

Braddock stepped over to him. He leaned down and could see that Milo was still breathing. He stood up straight when he heard clapping off to the side.

"Bravo," Miller called. Richards was smiling and nodding.

Braddock now had time to concentrate on just how hard his heart was pounding, and he took deep breaths. He dabbed at the gash on his cheek, grimacing when his fingers made contact.

Richards approached him. "You should see Doc Anderson about that cut," he said. "It's a beauty."

Braddock nodded. "Yeah, I think I will. Maybe even needs to be sewn back in place."

Miller joined them and bent over Milo to look at the man's head and the hole in his stable wall.

"Sorry about the wall," Braddock apologized.

"I'll fix it and tell you what it cost."

"Figures," Braddock said.

"You know, I think Milo's going to be even madder than he was before," Richards said. "I'm not sure he'll settle for just fists next time."

Braddock was thinking the same thing, but he didn't have an answer for that, other than to get out of town fast.

"Too bad the town doesn't have a marshal," Richards said. "Milo should be locked up until you're out of town."

Braddock smirked. "No deal."

Richards waved a hand at the unconscious gunman. "You handled that real well. You got a talent for being marshal."

"Just dumb luck." Braddock walked over to his gun belt and picked it up.

"If you were marshal, you could lock Milo up yourself. Or shoot him if he resisted."

Braddock walked over to Milo's gun belt. "I'm taking his gun," he said. "When he comes to, tell him I'm keeping it until I leave town. He can have it back then."

"But he'll just get another."

"Probably just buy one from Taylor's general store," Braddock said.

"Look, Mr. Braddock, as marshal you'll have a horse, so you can find your own horse easier. And you'll have an easier time dealing with McIntyre when you go to get your horse back."

"I'd be the marshal just of the town," Braddock said. "The ranches would be outside my jurisdiction."

Richards smiled. "Oh, we play pretty loose with those kinds of things around here. Always done it that way."

Braddock stared at Milo lying with his head in the barn. He was sure he would have to face that gunslinger again if he didn't get out of town fast. And the next time they met, Milo would probably just open fire on sight.

If only he hadn't stopped in Green Valley. If only he'd minded his own business. If only Sally Anderson hadn't walked past that saloon at that moment.

"I'm going to see the doctor," Braddock said.

Braddock carried Milo's gun belt in his left hand and kept his bandanna pressed against the gash in his cheek with his right.

Sally opened the door and looked at the bloody bandanna. "Oh, my," she said. "What happened to you?" She motioned him to come in.

He entered and she closed the door behind him. He set Milo's gun belt down on a chair.

"Whose is that?" she asked.

"Milo's. I took it away from him."

She gently removed the bandanna from the wound. She sucked in a little breath. "Did he do this to you?"

"Yes."

"Before or after you took his gun away from him?"

"Before."

She looked closer. "Did he use a knife?"

"No. Just his fist. What does it matter?" he snapped.

"I want your father to look at it. I think maybe the cut should be sewed shut."

"You're right. Unfortunately, my father isn't here. He was called out to the McCalls'. She's having a baby, and he could be gone the rest of the day or longer."

"Oh," Braddock said in disappointment. He pressed the cloth against the wound again. "Well, guess I'll go." But he didn't know where he would go.

"I can sew that wound for you."

He looked at her in surprise. "You can? Have you ever done this kind of thing before?"

"Did half the work on Wes Carter."

"Really? How is he, anyway?"

She nodded toward the inner room next to the operating room. "Still sleeping. Fever has set in. Not surprising in cases like this." She took him by an arm and led him to a straight chair, which she pulled away from the wall. ''You just sit here.'' She took off his hat and laid it on the table next to the chair. ''Try to relax.'' She headed for the other room. ''I'll get the needle.''

Braddock shuddered at the word. ''I don't know. Maybe I should wait until your father gets back,'' he called after her. He got back up, and when she didn't answer he picked up his hat and put it on. He still held the bandanna to his cheek. ''Look, Miss Anderson,'' he called, ''I'll come back later.''

''Later won't do you any good, Mr. Braddock,'' she answered from the other room. ''That wound needs attention now.''

She was back in about a minute with a large cloth draped over her shoulder. In one hand she was carrying a basin with water and a cloth hanging over the side. In the other hand she held a pair of scissors and a curved needle. A long thread hung from its eye. She stopped short when she saw him standing.

He took a step back when his eyes caught sight of the needle. ''Really, I—''

Sally smiled and started forward again. ''Now, I can't work on you standing up, sir.'' She laid the basin and needle down on the table, and then snatched Braddock's hat from his head and set it back down on the table. She placed her hands on his shoulders and pushed down gently. ''Down you go.''

He slowly sank to the chair. He looked over at the needle lying on the table.

Sally smiled. "Come on, Mr. Braddock. I'm sure you've been in a lot worse pain than this will be. The needle is very sharp. You'll hardly feel it. In fact, the bruise from the blow itself has probably numbed much of the area over the cheekbone."

Braddock looked up at her. "Well, if you say so."

Sally laid the cloth over his shoulder and tucked it into his collar. "That'll catch any more blood, but I'm afraid your shirt collar is already ruined." Then she gently pulled at his bandanna.

Braddock let it go reluctantly. He still had his eyes on her face. "How long will it take?" His heart was racing.

"About a minute. Just needs a couple of stitches."

He nodded slightly. "Well, okay."

She then dunked the other cloth into the water and wrung it out slightly. "This, on the other hand, may hurt a little. I have to get the dirt out of the wound."

"Okay." He clenched his teeth at the pain as she washed the wound out gently.

"Not much dirt in here," she said. "There." She dropped the cloth in the basin and picked up the needle with its thread. "You must hold perfectly still. If you flinch, you may rip the skin even more."

Sally used the fingers of her left hand to pinch the edges of the wound together. She used her right hand to puncture the skin with the needle.

Braddock was surprised. "You were right, Miss Anderson. I hardly felt that at all."

She smiled and kept working.

No longer apprehensive about the needle, he shifted his attention to her hand on his cheek. "You have nice hands," he said. "I mean, nice and steady hands. And you work quickly too."

"Thank you. Father says I would make a good surgeon."

"A woman as a doctor?" Braddock said. "Don't be ridiculous."

The needle plunged into his wound. He let out a yelp, and his body jerked at the unexpected pain. He spun his head round and glared at her. She had let go of the needle.

She smiled at him. "You flinched. I told you *not* to flinch."

"You did that on purpose," he said. He could tell the difference between a smile and smirk.

"Do you want me to stop?" she asked, still smiling.

Sitting there with a needle dangling from the end of thread running through his cheek, he knew that that would be silly. He turned away again. "Finish it," he said.

When she didn't start again, he looked at her. She was standing with her arms folded, still smiling smugly at him. She started tapping a foot.

"Please," he urged.

"That's better." She went back to work and was soon finished. She cut the end of the thread with the scissors.

"The wound is closed, but it's still bleeding," she informed him. "Just keep sitting there for a while until it stops.'' She picked up his bandanna and handed it to him. ''Keep this pressed gently against the wound.''

''Thank you,'' he said. She picked up her things and headed for the other room. ''I mean, thank you, doctor,'' he added with a smile.

She smiled again as she left the room, but this time it was with warmth.

Braddock settled back in the chair and looked at Milo's gun belt. His cheek was throbbing. But he was sure the pain would be worse if he and Milo ever met up again.

When Sally reentered the room, he looked up at her. ''What do I owe you for this, doctor?''

''I think you have enough problems already,'' she said. She walked over to him and peeked briefly under the bandanna. ''It's slowing already. Just sit here a little while longer.'' She sat down at a nearby chair. ''Any luck finding out about your horse yet?''

''Nope.'' He took a deep breath and let it out slowly. ''And the livery stable won't rent me a horse to go look for him.''

''Father has our only horse with the buggy out at the McCalls', otherwise, I'd let you use that. And as I said, Father could take a whole day or even two to get back.''

Braddock nodded appreciatively. ''That's very kind of you.''

''Have you considered just leaving town without your horse? Just taking the next stage out?''

''I've had Nick for more than three years now. Nice

gelding, great horse. We make a good team, and where I come from, you don't break up a good team.''

"That makes sense, but you may not get your horse back, no matter what," she said. "And you could get another horse if you had to."

"But not my gear and belongings. Nick had all of it in his saddlebags. Including the rest of my money. And if I don't get some more money, I can't go anywhere, stage or no stage."

She nodded thoughtfully. "What about Milo? He's the head gunfighter McIntyre hired, the meanest of them all. Looks like you've made a real enemy of him, and he'll come back."

"I know."

"I'll talk to Father as soon as he gets back. Maybe he'd even go with you to McIntyre. McIntyre respects him, and he might be able to help."

"Thanks. It may come to that." Braddock stood up. "In the meantime, I've got to try to find some other way of getting Nick back." He picked up his hat and put it on.

Sally stood up too. "Wait, let me check that wound." She came over and took away the bandanna and peered closely.

Braddock could feel her breath on his cheek, and he leaned slightly toward her. He tried not to shiver when she ran a fingertip lightly over the wound.

"It's stopped bleeding. But do be careful. It could start again if you're rough with the wound."

"I understand."

"And the stitches should come out in a few days."

"I hope I won't be here in a few days." He continued to look at her face, her eyes, her smooth complexion. "Not that I wouldn't like to stay in Green Valley a little longer," he added.

She smiled. "Be sure to stop back. I mean, so I can check on my patient."

He smiled and nodded. "Thank you, doctor, I will." He stepped across the room and picked up Milo's gun belt.

She held out his blood-soaked bandanna. "Do you want this?"

He sighed, took it from her, and stuffed it into his back pocket. "I may need it again."

He tipped his hat and left the office. Sally stood in the doorway and watched him till he was all the way down at the end of the street.

He stopped at the main street and searched both ways until he spotted the Green Valley Bank. He walked down to it and entered.

Richards sat at a desk in the rear of the bank, working on some papers. As Braddock approached, Richards laid his pen down and started to smile. "Good afternoon," he said.

Braddock took a deep breath and let it out slowly. "Mr. Richards . . ." he said simply.

Richards opened his desk drawer and reached inside. "Nice to see you again, Marshal Braddock," he said. He laid a shiny tin star on the desktop.

Chapter Four

Braddock opened the door of the marshal's office and looked around the room. It was Spartan, with only a desk, a couple of chairs, a stove, and a cot along one wall. There were a few shelves above the cot, and there was a gun rack along the opposite wall. It held several Winchesters and a shotgun, all secured with a chain and a lock. Through a narrow door in the wall directly across from him, he could see some jail cells.

He stepped in, closed the door slowly, and strolled over to the desk and plopped down in the swivel chair. He swiveled back and forth a couple of times. He felt completely out of place. And plenty worried.

The door opened with a flourish and Josh Miller burst inside. "Well, Lee's leeches," he blurted with a big smile. "Marshal, huh? You know what you're doin'?"

Braddock shook his head forlornly. "I've done some dumb things in my life," he admitted, "but this may be the dumbest." He looked down at the metal emblem on his vest. "And it's not even a real badge."

"Nope," Miller said. "Cut it out of the bottom of

51

a tin can myself, and then soldered a pin on it." He started toward the cell area.

"What are you here for?" Braddock asked.

"Richards told me you were the new town marshal. Town pays me to keep the place clean. And I also furnish the horse and gear." Miller squinted at Braddock's face. "What's that on your cheek?"

"Stitches. Where Milo hit me."

"I thought I saw Doc drive out of town earlier today."

"You did. His daughter did this."

Miller raised an eyebrow. "Sherman's shirt, Marshal! You let a woman do that to you, like she was darning a sock?"

Braddock scowled at him. "Yes, and she did a first-class job of it too."

"Okay, okay, it's your hide." Miller disappeared for a few moments and then returned with a broom and started to sweep. "'Course," he said, "the place hasn't had much time to get too dirty. Marshal Tate hasn't been gone that long."

"Don't remind me," Braddock said. "But I won't be staying long myself. Just till I get my horse and gear back. Don't care about my money if it's gone."

"Richards give you some pay in advance?" Miller asked.

"Yes, more than I had when I came to town."

"Well, you'll earn it."

Miller was sweeping up a cloud of dust at the front of the office, but he was merely rearranging the dirt.

Braddock opened the desk drawer and shuffled through its contents. "You know where the marshal kept the keys to the long guns?"

As Miller opened the door, a breeze stirred up the dust again. "Upper right-hand drawer," he told Braddock.

Braddock opened the specified drawer, picked up a heavy ring with a few keys on it, and stood up. He shook his head at Miller's trying to sweep dirt out the front door into the wind.

Next he went over to the gun rack, unlocked the chain, and took out a Winchester. After locking the chain again, he put the key ring back in the drawer.

"What are you up to?" Miller asked. While he rested on the broom handle in the open doorway, the wind blew the dust back into the office.

"Where's Milo?" Braddock asked.

Miller laughed. "At the moment he's soaking his head in a bucket of water at my stable." He walked up to Braddock, who was now shoving cartridges into the magazine of the Winchester. "But he said he's comin' after you when his head stops hurtin'."

"Figured that."

"What are going to do about it?"

"Well, where I come from, we try to avoid trouble by meeting it head-on."

Miller frowned. "You gonna shoot it out with him?"

Braddock headed for the door. "I sure hope not. And I'm going to need a horse as soon as I get back."

"Okay, Marshal," Miller said. Then he added quickly, "Oh, Marshal?"

Braddock stopped. "Yes?"

"Fixin' the barn will cost two dollars, I figure."

Braddock looked disgusted. "Charge it to the town. Marshal's expenses." He left and banged the door shut behind him.

Miller shrugged. "In that case, it'll cost five dollars." He started whistling as he went back to sweeping.

Braddock walked down the street toward the livery stable. He carried the Winchester casually in his right hand, and people stared at him. A few nodded. One even said, "'Afternoon, Marshal." Braddock got the impression that people had actually come out to wait for him, to see the new marshal. They were curious about the man who would be foolhardy enough to put on a badge in Green Valley at this time.

He glanced at the crowd standing on the boardwalk in front of the Golden Riches saloon across the street. Hanson was in front, his thumbs hooked in his gun belt. When their eyes met, Hanson lifted one hand and lightly tapped the brim of his hat in a salute. Braddock noticed that Hanson wasn't smiling, but he didn't think the man was impressed with the badge. Perhaps it was a show of respect for his courage. Braddock merely nodded acknowledgment.

Braddock reached the stable and, raising the Winchester, he entered slowly. The sound of water splashing came from the room off to the side. He approached the room cautiously.

Milo was sitting on a low stool with his head hanging over a wooden bucket on the floor. He was scooping water up with a bandanna and slopping it over his head. He was facing the door.

"How's your head, Milo?" Braddock asked.

Milo's head snapped up, but he grimaced in pain. Then he glared at Braddock, his teeth clenched. A rising growl filled the room. He leaped to his feet.

Braddock swung the carbine to point at Milo, and he cocked the hammer. The big man stopped short. "You just threatened an officer of the law, Milo."

"What are you talkin' about, Braddock?"

"*Marshal* Braddock to you." Braddock tapped the badge on his vest with a thumb. "You're under arrest."

Milo's mouth dropped open in astonishment. He put his hands on his hips. "You're kiddin'."

Braddock glanced at Milo's hip. At least Milo hadn't had time to get another pistol yet. "You want to lose an arm like Wes?"

"You mean you're just going to stand there and shoot me?"

"For resisting arrest. This badge is for real, and you're really under arrest. If you resist, I'll shoot you. You decide." Milo studied him closely while he continued. "You'd spend about a day in a cell until I get my horse back and leave town. Decide now. I'm in a hurry. What'll it be—jail or a bullet?" Braddock waited. Milo waited. So Braddock fired a round into the bucket. The wooden slats exploded into slivers.

Milo's hands came up quickly. "All right, all right. Don't get an itchy finger."

Braddock levered another cartridge into the Winchester's chamber and backed up. "Let's move."

Milo slowly picked up his hat. He grimaced as the movement made his head throb anew. He didn't put the hat on, but merely carried it in his hand. He glared at Braddock as he moved past him, but Braddock kept well out of his reach.

They headed along the boardwalk toward the marshal's office. Spectators stood quietly and watched the two men advance. Braddock saw Hanson slowly crossing the street. His hands swung casually at his sides. Hanson stopped at the edge of the boardwalk.

"We heard a shot," Hanson said. "What are you doing?"

Braddock and Milo stopped on the boardwalk. "This man's under arrest for attacking the town marshal," Braddock told Hanson. "He's going to spend a little time in a cell."

Hanson nodded. "I see."

Milo snorted. "It's gonna be a mighty short time," he said.

Josh Miller approached just then from the other direction on the boardwalk. "Well, Grant's gravy. You take this job seriously, don't you?"

Braddock poked Milo in the back with the barrel of the Winchester. "Move."

Miller stepped aside. Braddock kept his eyes on Milo, but he said, "Josh, bring the horse up to the office."

"Yes, sir, Mr. Marshal."

Milo started walking again. He glared at Miller and then looked back at Hanson. "Braddock here could be a real nuisance," he said.

Hanson smiled as he watched Braddock and Milo clump their way up the boardwalk. Miller gawked at the two as they receded. When Hanson said, "The marshal wants you to get his horse ready," Miller jumped and headed up the boardwalk.

In the marshal's office, Braddock fished the ring of keys out of the desk drawer again and then led Milo into the cell area, keeping the Winchester ready. "Take your pick," he said.

Milo entered a cell, threw his hat on the cot, and then sat down. He glared at Braddock as the iron door closed with a clank. Braddock tried one of the two larger keys on the ring. It was the wrong key, and he had to switch to the other one.

"Might as well leave it unlocked," Milo said. "I'm not gonna be here long. I've got friends."

"If you mean McIntyre, I'm going out to see him right now. We can talk about you then."

Back in the office, Braddock tossed the keys into the drawer and slammed it shut. Then the door opened and Sally Anderson walked in. She was carrying a basket covered with a white cloth.

"Hello, Marshal," she said with a smile.

"What brings you here?"

"Supper."

Braddock's eyebrows went up. "Oh?"

"Mr. Richards told me you've taken the job of marshal. I always cook for the marshal and his prisoners, though I didn't know that you already have one." She nodded toward Milo.

"I want to know he's where he can't plug me in the back."

"Sensible," Sally said. "Always sensible." She put the basket down on the desk and took off the cloth.

"I hadn't realized it was so late in the day already."

"It'll be dusk in a couple of hours."

Braddock looked down into the basket, which contained bread and slabs of beef, two hard-boiled eggs, a large piece of cheese, a china plate, utensils, a small coffeepot, and a cup. "I had forgotten about food coming with the job," he said. "This all looks wonderful."

"Thank you." She carefully drew out each item from the basket and set it on the desktop. "Please, sit down, Marshal."

"You bet," he said eagerly. He leaned the carbine against the desk and then took off his hat and placed it on the desk to one side. He started to sit down, but then stopped and motioned to a chair in front of the desk. "Won't you join me, please, Miss Anderson?" he asked.

"Thank you," she said, and pulled the chair a little closer and sat down. "I've already eaten, though."

He sat down and quickly dished up the food. "How

about just some coffee, then? There must be another cup around here somewhere.''

''No, thank you.''

He started eating. ''It's delicious,'' he said. ''Deee-licious. I haven't tasted anything as good as this even back where I come from.''

Sally smiled. ''Maybe it's all the dust. How are the stitches?''

''Oh, fine, fine.'' He tore off a chunk of the bread and bit off a large piece. ''This tastes freshly baked. It's wonderful.''

The door opened and Josh Miller came in. ''Got your horse, Marshal,'' he said on his way to the desk.

''That was fast,'' Braddock said.

''Uh-huh. Saddle, scabbard, canteen, and lariat. Didn't know if you wanted a bedroll, but I could—'' He whistled when he saw Braddock's meal. ''Burn-side's britches,'' he said. ''Tate never got a meal like that. Just beans and—''

Sally glared at him. ''Don't you have some work to do, Josh?''

''What?'' Miller said in surprise.

Braddock saw the glare. Miller looked at Sally, then at Braddock, who had stopped chewing, and then back at Sally. She cleared her throat.

''Oh, yep, sure enough, Miss Sally.'' Miller started backing to the door. ''Say, Marshal, don't suppose you know anything about the bucket in my stable?''

Braddock shifted the lump of food in his mouth. ''I did it, Josh. The town will—''

"You bet," Miller said, smiling. "Marshal's expenses." He left.

Braddock looked at Sally, but she lowered her eyes. He couldn't suppress a smile. He started chewing again, and pondering. "Has your father come back yet?"

Sally looked up again. "No, but that's not unexpected. Babies can be pretty uncooperative."

"Yes, bless them." He continued eating and finished up the last of the beef. "Beef is excellent."

"Well, actually, beef is about the same cost as beans right now, what with the drought and all the cattle on the market and a lot of them just going to waste dying out on the desert with nothing to eat or drink so that a person should—I mean—" She lowered her eyes and started to straighten her dress. "Well, it's just being frugal to—uh—"

"Oh, yes, I agree," Braddock said. "We do the same ourselves back where I come from." He was sure she was blushing.

Suddenly she rose. He jumped to his feet too, dropping his fork.

"I really must get back," Sally told him. "Father could be back at any time, and he's always pretty hungry after a long day like this."

"Even if he weren't, he'd get hungry real fast with food like this in the house."

Sally smiled. "I'll bring something back for your prisoner later."

"All right, but let me give it to him. I don't want him grabbing you or anything."

"Always sensible, Marshal Braddock."

"People who know me well just call me Clay, Miss Anderson. As marshal, I think I'm entitled to say how people address me."

She smiled and nodded slightly. "Clay," she said.

He smiled and waited, hoping that she would reciprocate.

She spoke slowly: "And why don't you just call me Sally?"

"A pleasure . . . Sally."

"Good night, Clay."

"Good night, Sally."

She opened the door and slipped outside with a swish of her dress. Braddock just stood there staring at the closed door.

"Braddock," Milo said from his cell.

Braddock looked back, irritated at the interruption. "What?"

Milo was standing with his hands draped through the bars. "You ain't gonna live long enough to see her again."

Chapter Five

Braddock kept Miller's horse at a fair canter. The critter was steady, responsive, and easy to ride. Braddock was eager to get to McIntyre's ranch as soon as he could, but he did not want to wear the horse out. It was still hot even though the sun was low in the sky.

Miller had said that the ranch would be easy to find—just follow the road east for about twelve miles. Since the ranch stretched clear across the whole eastern end of the valley, the road led right to his place.

While riding, Braddock couldn't shake the feeling that he was being stupid. Maybe he should forget about Nick and his saddle and just use the mayor's advance to buy a horse and saddle and take off for Montana while he was still alive.

But there were some things in his saddlebags that couldn't be replaced the way a horse or a saddle could. Mementos, a picture of his parents, his father's straight-edge razor, and the lucky sailor's button that his grandfather had given to him as a little boy. He couldn't remember what his grandfather looked like, but he remembered clearly the day he'd gotten the button, which looked like just a button.

Ah, but there was Sally Anderson too. What would he do if he found Nick and his things? He was powerfully attracted to the pretty and capable young woman. And he was sure he hadn't misinterpreted her behavior at the marshal's office; she was attracted to him too. But how long could he stay in Green Valley, or how long should he stay? What would he do in Green Valley? Not continue as town marshal. That was for sure. And what would his sister do up along the Yellowstone?

He sighed. Best not to think too hard, and to simply get on with the job at hand.

Actually, he wasn't sure what he was going to find at McIntyre's. He had no reason to believe that Billy Stickle and Elmo Flick would take Nick there, or that the two men were even there themselves. For all he knew, they might have simply hidden Nick somewhere and were hiding out themselves until they could get revenge for the loss of Wes Carter's arm. If he found the men, though, he thought he could get Nick and his gear back. Or maybe get killed.

The sun was getting low on the horizon behind him, and it bathed the landscape ahead of him in a soft golden light that he had always found to be pleasant and warm. It was light that allowed all the colors of the land to stand out in sharp contrast, not be washed out in the blinding yellow glare of the daytime sun.

Of course, there was hardly anything green to show except for some scraggly greasewood and some cactus. Almost everything was covered with dust, and the colors he could see were mostly shades of yellow, tan, and brown.

What pained him most was the sight of the cattle carcasses. No matter where he was along the road, he could always see at least one dead cow on the desert floor. Some looked fresh, and there were vultures nearby or sitting on carcasses and feeding. The vultures didn't have thermals to ride anymore that late in the day, and so he saw few of them in the air. And most of the other birds had already gone to roost for the night.

And then there were the doomed but still living cattle. They stood in one place, their ribs showing, heads hanging, tongues out, a hopeless glaze to their eyes. It all tugged at Braddock's heart. He didn't love cows particularly, but he did love cow country, and you couldn't have one without the other.

He stopped the horse and reached for the canteen. He pulled out the cork and took a long, deep, satisfying drink. Then he squinted at a dust cloud. It was a band of riders, and they were pounding fast in his direction.

Given the situation in the valley and the badge on his vest, the riders were not a welcome sight. But maybe they weren't seeking him. At any rate, he had no idea if Miller's horse could outrun them. So he waited.

There were a dozen riders, and they slowed a bit when they saw him waiting for them. He turned his horse to face them, and they pulled up just a few feet in front of him. The horses were breathing hard and their sides heaved. None of the animals could stand still after their hard ride. He saw Tyler Hanson, Jim Wells, and Dave Reever among the men.

"Gentlemen," Braddock said. He kept his right hand near his pistol, but he knew that any action would be futile against this many men.

"Are you Marshal Braddock?" a big man in front asked.

"I am."

"I'm Judson Davis."

"I've heard of you," Braddock said. Davis reminded him of Milo to some extent. His body shape was about the same, but the hair that stuck out from underneath his hat was gray, and his face was square and hard. Huge hands made his horse's reins seem like sewing threads.

Davis waved a hand to his left. "These are my sons, Harlan and Randy. And that's my top hand, Lowell Sperry."

The three men nodded and Braddock nodded back. Harlan had somewhat the build of his father, but he had black hair and a beard of black stubble. Randy was much slimmer, and his complexion was fair and his hair light brown.

Sperry was lean and tough-looking, the kind of appearance that comes from many years on the range in hot, dry cow country. Braddock had the feeling that Sperry did twice the work of the two Davis boys together.

Davis then nodded to his other side. "Hanson says you've already met him and his boys."

"Yes. Hello, Hanson." Davis didn't say anything about the four other men with him, but Braddock thought that the two behind Hanson were gunfighters while the three behind Sperry had to be cowhands. Braddock noticed that the gunfighters and cowhands had automatically separated themselves from each other. It said a lot about both kinds of men.

"Hello, Braddock," Hanson said. "Told Mr. Davis about you. He wanted to have a talk with you."

"Oh?" Braddock looked at Davis. "What about?"

"Well, from what Hanson told me about the way you handled McIntyre's hired killer, Milo, I think you ought to be working for me."

Braddock thought it best not to comment about *Davis's* hired killer. "I've got another job," he said.

"So I heard." Davis nodded toward the tin star. "You going to arrest Douglas McIntyre for the murder of my son?"

"Seems that there is a difference of opinion about his guilt, Mr. Davis."

"Mayor Richards saw him do it," Davis said. "That's good enough for us."

Davis's sons and all the cowhands nodded. The gunfighters made no response. "I've heard there are witnesses who say Doug McIntyre couldn't have done it," Braddock said.

"All of 'em work for McIntyre!" Davis snapped. "What do you expect them to say?"

"Maybe a jury ought to try to decide who's telling the truth."

"You arrest him," Davis said, "and I'll get you your jury."

All Davis men, no doubt, Braddock thought. But he was in kind of a trap. He was marshal and was supposed to be upholding the law, even if his reason for taking the job had been to get Nick back.

"I'll have a talk with McIntyre," he said.

Davis snorted. "Talk! What's there to talk about? One way or another, Douglas McIntyre is going to swing for the murder of my son and *their* brother." He poked a finger at his two sons as he mentioned them. Harlan and Randy both nodded vigorously.

"He killed my brother and he's going to die for it!" Randy shouted.

"Be quiet!" his father snapped. "I'll do the talking."

"I understand how you feel," Braddock said. "But I have to hear both sides, take a look at all the evidence."

"All you need to do is to talk to Richards," Davis said. "And I've already done that."

"Nevertheless, if you want Doug McIntyre arrested, you have to let me do it my way."

Hanson leaned forward and his saddle leather creaked. "We don't expect you to arrest him all by yourself."

"That's right," Davis said. "We'll back you up. That's why we're here."

Braddock figured that McIntyre would have as many men, and that his tin star might make the handiest target in a shootout. "I still need to talk to McIntyre first," he said. And if he could find Nick and his gear, he could forget about Doug McIntyre entirely.

"We're losing patience!" Davis roared. "We're going to just ride in there and take him ourselves pretty soon."

"Not without a lot of men getting killed, you won't," Braddock said. He could see boiling frustration on Davis's face. He realized that although Davis was surely a hard man, he was not stupid, and not, apparently, completely ruthless. "Maybe even your other two sons," he added.

Davis jabbed a finger at Braddock. "All right! You talk to McIntyre. But time's running out!" He waved a hand, kicked his horse hard, and turned and rode off. The other men followed.

Braddock sighed. This was a situation in which there were no good solutions. More men were going to die before this was settled. He hoped he could find Nick quickly and head for the Yellowstone. He gave Miller's horse a kick and rode on.

McIntyre's ranch buildings were impressive. The main house was made of stone and lumber and gave an aura of strength and permanence that even the drought couldn't weaken. There were several barns and stables, and the entire ranch setting was surrounded by large corrals with horses. A few smaller corrals held segregated bulls. McIntyre was going to make sure his bulls made it through the drought.

Braddock also noted that there was a large body of men standing about in the middle of the ranch yard. Some of them held saddled horses. He couldn't see clearly in the gathering dusk, but there seemed to be an argument going on.

He glanced at the horses in the nearest corral, brought Miller's horse to a sudden stop, and stood up in the stirrups. "Nick!" he shouted.

His longtime companion raised his head from nibbling at parched grass. The horse snuffled.

Braddock whistled, sat back down in the saddle, and kicked his mount toward the corral fence. "Here, boy, come on."

Nick sniffed at the wind and started walking forward and then broke into a trot. He reached Braddock, who stretched a hand over the fence and patted him on the neck affectionately. "Thought I'd never see you again," Braddock said, smiling. "Didn't think it would be this easy to find you, either." And it was a troubling thought. Why no attempt to hide the stolen horse?

As he heard horses coming his way, he looked toward the ranch buildings and saw three riders pounding toward him. Men in the courtyard were staring at him. He directed Miller's horse away from the fence.

As the three men brought their horses to a halt in front of him, they were surprised to see his badge.

They looked young and angry, but he didn't think any of them was McIntyre.

"Who are you?" the man in front asked.

"Clay Braddock's my name." He nodded toward Nick. "That's my horse, and I've come to take him back."

The three men looked at one another. The man in front spoke again: "We wondered if Billy and Elmo really got that horse in a poker game."

"I want to talk to them," Braddock said. "They also took my saddle and gear."

"They went back to town. Didn't you pass them coming up the road?"

Braddock was disappointed. "No."

The man in front pointed at the tin star. "You really a marshal?"

"The badge says I am. And who are you?"

"Douglas McIntyre."

"Is that right?" Braddock studied the man carefully. Was this man a killer? He was a big, strong, handsome man, with muscles that rippled under his shirt. Braddock was struck by Doug's hat. It was an ordinary hat, but it had two silver conchos pinned to the band on the right side. Odd ornaments so far north of the Navajo nation.

"You're on my father's land, which I suppose you know," Doug said.

Braddock nodded. "If Billy and Elmo aren't here, I want to talk to your father."

"He'll probably want to talk to you too. If you're really the law, we've got some business for you."

Uh-oh, Braddock thought. "Lead on."

Doug and his two men whirled round their horses and set off at a gallop for the ranch. Braddock followed more slowly. By the time he reached the courtyard, Doug had already dismounted and was talking to an older man standing there.

Braddock rode up. It was then that he noticed the body of a man stretched out on the ground. Nearby, two other men were having wounds cared for. They both showed blood on their clothes, but they were sitting up on the low wall that surrounded a dead tree.

Braddock studied the older man. He wore no hat, and he looked like he had just come out of the house. He was bald and slightly stoop-shouldered, but his stomach was still flat. The other men in the courtyard clustered around him.

"Are you Angus McIntyre?" Braddock asked.

"I am," the older man said proudly.

"What happened here?"

McIntyre pointed to the body. "Davis's men did that."

A cowhand spoke up. "It was that Hanson and some of his hired guns. They jumped us about an hour ago. We left another man dead back on the plateau. Sam here just died."

"This is Ned Early, my top hand," McIntyre said. "I'd trust him with my life. If he says Hanson and his boys did it, then Hanson and his boys did it. And what are you going to do about it, Marshal?'' McIntyre emphasized the title.

Braddock paused. Before, he'd been trying to avoid having to fight McIntyre and his men. But McIntyre had now put him on the other side of the fence. ''It didn't happen in town, so it's sort of out of my jurisdiction,'' he said tentatively.

Doug thrust out an angry finger at Braddock. ''I told you he was probably working for Davis! I knew it.''

McIntyre looked at Braddock and squinted. ''Maybe you'd better just ride out of here, mister.''

Instead, Braddock slowly dismounted. ''You've got my horse, Mr. McIntyre,'' he said. ''I want him and my gear back.''

''What are you talking about?''

Doug said, ''That horse Billy and Elmo brought in earlier.''

''Thought they won that in a poker game,'' Early said.

''They stole it,'' Braddock corrected him.

''Not very bright to steal a marshal's horse,'' McIntyre said.

''I wasn't the marshal when they stole it.''

''Well, I don't think you're going to be marshal very long,'' McIntyre informed him. ''If you won't help us, then you'd better get out of the way. Killing my men was the last straw. I've tried to be reasonable for years now, but Davis wants a war and I'm going to give him one. And no marshal is going to stop me!''

"Davis says Doug here killed his son," Braddock said. "Sounds to me like maybe *you* started the war."

McIntyre screamed at him: "He didn't kill Earl Davis! Nor did any of my men! Richards is blind!"

"Said it was me and one of Davis's own men, Willard Pyle, that did it," Doug said. "Well, it wasn't me."

Early stepped forward. "I swear that Doug was with me here when Earl was killed. And I got ten other men who can say the same thing."

"Then let's have a trial," Braddock said. "With your witnesses, no jury would convict Doug. Where I come from, a man has to be proved guilty. And what about this other man, Willard Pyle? Nobody mentioned him to me before."

"He conveniently disappeared," Doug muttered. He said something else in disgust and turned away.

McIntyre shook his head in disbelief. "Do you think I'd hand my son over to a jury hired by Davis?"

Braddock thought that McIntyre's suspicions were probably well justified. "Well, have the trial somewhere else," he suggested. "Where no one knows either of you."

"If that jury didn't hang Douglas, Davis would, anyway," McIntyre said. "Judson Davis recognizes no law but his own. He cheated me out of land when we first came to this valley. He's stolen my cattle, trampled my grain, ruined my water, and run off my men. And now he's killing them. He wants to have this ranch, but he'll have to kill me first."

"From what I saw coming up here, there's not going to be much ranch to be had."

"We can make it," McIntyre said.

"Your stock won't. Why don't you slaughter most of them and keep the rest healthy?"

"There's no market for beef."

"Just kill them, then. They're going to die, anyway."

"And let Davis's cattle take over the range and water?" McIntyre said angrily. "And then where would I be? Crowded out, and with no cattle, no money. The bank would foreclose on the ranch and sell it to Davis cheap."

"But isn't he in the same cactus patch as you?"

McIntyre laughed sarcastically. "Davis owns most of the stock in the bank. Are you going to stand there and tell me you didn't know that?"

"I *didn't* know that," Braddock said.

McIntyre snickered. "You got grit, Marshal. I'll say that for you."

"It's the truth, Mr. McIntyre."

"No matter. Davis has Richards on his side. And the other men in town too—Bennett and Taylor and the rest." McIntyre stepped closer and peered into Braddock's face. "And what about you?" he asked slowly. "Why would anybody be dumb enough to take the job of town marshal in Green Valley at a time like this unless he were being paid handsomely to take sides against me?"

"I needed money and a horse, and it was the only

work I could get quick,'' Braddock said. ''And I'll promise you, if I get my horse and gear back, I'll be headed for Montana by morning.''

Doug and his father looked at each other.

Early laughed and said, ''Never heard of a marshal like you before.''

McIntyre looked back at Braddock. ''That's a very sensible thing to do,'' he said. ''Tomorrow I'm sending Douglas and Early and some men into Green Valley to round up all the hands and guns. Then we're going to get rid of Davis for good. It would be very healthy for you to be a good ways north of here by then.''

''How about my gear?'' Braddock asked.

McIntyre looked back. ''Anybody know about any gear that came with that horse Billy and Elmo brought in?''

''It's stacked in the north stable,'' Early said.

''Get it,'' McIntyre ordered. ''And bring Braddock his horse.''

Early motioned to some cowhands. Some went over to a stable, and two others headed for the corral. In a few minutes they were all back. They dumped a saddle and gear, a bedroll, saddlebags, a carbine, and other equipment on the ground. One cowhand held Nick by a halter.

Braddock knelt down, undid the straps of the saddlebags, and pawed his way through them. All his belongings were there except the money. He decided he would overlook the money. He stood up. ''All here,'' he said.

"Good," McIntyre said. "Get his horse saddled."

Several men fell on Braddock's saddle and gear, and they quickly had Nick saddled. Braddock took the reins and mounted.

He gave McIntyre a slight salute. "Much obliged."

"Have a nice ride, Marshal," McIntyre replied. There was derision in his voice.

Braddock grabbed the reins of Miller's horse and turned Nick. He started to leave, but then stopped and turned back to look at McIntyre and his son and Early. "There must be a better way," he said. "A lot of good men are about to be killed."

McIntyre shook his head. "If it's Davis or any of his men, they aren't good men."

Braddock slumped in the saddle a little. He said no more, just gave a Nick a little kick. Then he and the two horses left the ranch yard.

Within a short time it was dark. A slight moon was coming up, but even when it had risen high in the sky, it would not provide much light. However, the road back to town was easy to follow.

He gave Nick a pat on the neck. "Good to have you back, Nick, ol' boy," he said. "And just in time. By this time tomorrow night, I'm afraid there's going to be lead flying all over this valley, and wearing a badge will be no protection."

He cantered along for a while, but then slowed Nick to a walk. "Sure wish I had more time to think, Nick," he said. "The money's gone, but I got you and the rest of my things back. But what do I do about Sally

Anderson? She's the prettiest, boldest, friendliest, and most capable gal I ever met. None like her where we come from. And she likes me. I'm sure of it.''

Nick snorted, and Miller's horse, trailing a little to the right of Braddock at the end of the outstretched reins, whickered slightly. Braddock noticed Nick's ears cup forward.

Braddock tugged back on the reins, and Nick stopped. Miller's horse sidled up next to them and stopped. Braddock stared into the darkness down the road, then off to the sides, and then straight down the road ahead. He twisted his head to one side and then the other and listened carefully. He could see nothing unusual and hear nothing unusual. Yet he trusted his sixth sense, which told him that someone was waiting for him up ahead.

As Braddock peered into the night he slowly shifted the reins of Miller's horse to his left hand. Then he reached down for the butt of the Winchester in the saddle scabbard, hoping that the bushwhacker wasn't catching the movement.

He was wrong, and within seconds, rifle fire exploded on both sides ahead of him. A half dozen rounds were fired, muzzles flashed, and bullets whistled at him as the attackers tried to get him in the first volley.

Miller's horse dropped like a rock. Nick reared and whinnied, and Braddock tumbled off backward, his right hand clutching the carbine's stock. He landed awkwardly, knocking the breath out of himself. He rolled once and then lay still on his stomach, gasping silently, trying to suck in air.

He continued to lie still while trying to spot any sign of his assailants. Nick trotted off a few spaces and then stopped. Braddock shifted his hand to the grip and trigger of the Winchester and cocked the hammer. He waited.

All was quiet. No more shots came. He heard no one, and he didn't move. Finally Nick sauntered over to where Braddock lay and lowered his head to snuffle at him.

He couldn't decide whether to get up and run, or to shoo Nick away and do something else. Whatever he did, Nick's actions had identified his position for his attackers. Soon he heard scuffling and then whispering.

"But look at his horse, Elmo," someone said. "The guy must still be lying where he landed. I know we got him. Let's get out of here."

"Can't see him, though, Billy," came an answer. "He must have fallen in the sagebrush. We gotta make sure."

"Let's go, Elmo. We got him. I know we did."

"We gotta make sure," Elmo repeated angrily. "Boss will want to know."

"All right. Go take a look."

Braddock heard grumbling and then crunching footsteps coming closer. Nick raised his head and cocked his ears. Finally, Braddock spotted a dim figure in the dark. He used his left hand to raise the barrel of the Winchester a few inches off the ground. Then he fired.

The approaching man threw back his arms, flipped his carbine backward, and crashed to the ground.

Braddock leaped to his feet and scampered ten yards off to the side, levering a fresh cartridge into the Winchester's chamber as he ran. The other man swore and fired frantically into the night. Braddock didn't think the bullets came anywhere near him. Nick trotted away again.

Braddock flopped to the ground and held his breath to stop the panting from the sudden exertion. He heard the man running in the other direction, into the desert away from the road, probably for his horse.

Braddock leaped to his feet and took off in pursuit. It was somewhat blind at first, but then he caught sight of the shadowy figure. He slid to a stop and fired a round. The other man turned and fired back. Both men missed.

Braddock started running hard again. He now discerned the shape of a horse and the man trying frantically to mount. The agitated horse sidled away from him. Finally the man got into the saddle. He kicked hard at the horse, yelled, and took off in the direction away from Braddock.

Braddock stopped, raised the Winchester, and fired. He didn't wait to see the effect of his shot but just kept levering in new cartridges as fast he could fire them off.

At the fourth shot he heard the horse scream. At the fifth shot the horse and man went down. Braddock stopped firing and rushed forward, more cautiously this time. When he got close to where he thought the horse had gone down, he stopped and listened and searched with his eyes.

He could see the horse lying on its side. But he couldn't see the man.

He took a step forward and then another. Finally he saw the crumpled form about ten feet ahead of the horse's body. From the way the man was lying, Braddock was pretty sure he was badly hurt if not dead.

He approached carefully. But the man on the ground never moved. He bent over the figure and searched for signs of life. "Broken neck," he muttered, and looked down carefully at the man.

He stood up, puzzled. This ambush was not over Wes's lost arm. The two men had mentioned that their boss wanted Braddock dead. Yet Braddock had told McIntyre he would leave town immediately. Hadn't McIntyre believed him?

Braddock walked back toward the road, and found the other man lying in the middle of it. He bent over and heard the man's raspy, bubbly breath, which meant blood in the lungs.

He knelt beside the man and felt over his chest and found the wound.

The man spoke: "Good shot, Marshal." His voice was soft.

Braddock didn't know what to say. There was no sign of anger in the words or tone. "You tried to kill me," he said.

"Thought I had," Elmo said.

"You got Miller's horse instead."

The man chuckled but stopped quickly. "Too dark."

There was silence for a while. Braddock listened to Elmo's labored breathing. "I can't take you to town on horseback," he said. "I'll send a wagon back for you. Get you to Dr. Anderson." But he knew the doctor couldn't help Elmo.

Elmo also knew it. He shook his head a little. "Too late. I'm gone. I've seen wounds like this before."

Braddock didn't really feel sorry for the man. How many men had this dying man killed? And Braddock had only defended himself. "Why did McIntyre want me killed? I was leaving, anyway."

There was silence for a while. "McIntyre? Well, the boss has lots more men, Braddock. You'll be dead by tomorrow night this time."

Braddock stood up. "Thanks for the warning." Now he was sure he should leave town immediately, Sally or no Sally. "What do you want me to do for you?" he asked.

"Leave me be," Elmo said. "It's a good night for dying."

Braddock was pretty sure too that Elmo wouldn't see the dawn. "All right."

He walked down the road to where Nick was standing near Miller's dead horse. He replaced the Winchester in the saddle scabbard and mounted. Then he walked Nick over to the dying man and stopped. "Anything I can do to make you comfortable?"

"You got any whiskey?" Elmo managed to rasp out.

"Sorry, no." Braddock looked down at Elmo a little longer. He couldn't see his face but could hear his hard breathing. He glanced into the darkness on the other side of the road. Another man lay out there already dead. He didn't feel guilty for what he had done, but he didn't feel good about it, either. What if he hadn't stopped for beans at the Desert Hole earlier?

He gave Nick a little nudge and headed for town.

Chapter Six

Braddock walked Nick down the dark street to the livery stable. The light from its big open barn doors flooded a large patch of ground in front. He heard someone pounding a hammer inside.

Standing in the doorway, Richards watched him approach and then threw his arms wide. "Braddock!" he called. "You're back!"

Braddock wasn't sure whether Richards was happy to see him or astonished to see him. Given the life expectancy of a marshal in Green Valley, he figured it was the latter.

He stopped in the patch of light. "Yes, and this is Nick." He patted his horse on the neck. "I got my horse back."

"I've been looking for you," Richards said.

Braddock dismounted. "And I've been looking for you." He unpinned the badge from his vest, grasped Richards' hand, and turned it palm up. He slapped the badge into the hand. "I quit."

Richards looked down at the tin star, dumbfounded. "What?"

"I got my horse, my gear, and my belongings, and

I'm heading for Montana first thing in the morning."
He led Nick into the stable. Miller was kneeling and
pounding nails into a large box he was fashioning on
the dusty, straw-covered floor.

Richards hurried after Braddock and said, "I've got
to talk to you."

Braddock waved him off. "I won't change my
mind."

Miller looked up. "Howdy, Marshal," he said.
Then he picked up another nail and drove it into the
board he was working on.

"Found my horse. I want to put him up for the
night."

"Sure." Miller looked up again, past Braddock.
"But where's *my* horse?"

"Lying dead on the McIntyre road."

"Mead's mother!" Miller looked up at him, but the
expression of shock quickly faded. "Marshal's ex-
pense?"

Braddock nodded and smiled, but he noticed that
Miller wasn't smiling. He pointed to the box. "Is that
a coffin you're building there?"

Miller drove a final nail into the board and stood up.
"A coffin it is." He stepped over to a pile of lumber
in the rear stall, selected a board, and pulled it out.

"Well, you'll need two more," Braddock said.

"Oh?"

"There are two dead men out near your dead horse.
Take a wagon out there tomorrow morning and pick
them up."

"Two men?" Richards came up closer. "What happened?"

"Billy Stickle and Elmo Flick tried to bushwhack me."

"Those are McIntyre's men," Miller said.

"Were McIntyre's men," Braddock corrected him. "I think McIntyre sent them out to kill me because he wasn't sure I'd really leave in the morning. This range war is really going to explode tomorrow, and I guess he didn't want me around."

"Tomorrow? Why do you say that?" Miller asked.

"Hanson and his boys killed two of McIntyre's men."

"I see," Richards said.

Miller looked at the stack of lumber. "Guess I should have ordered more boards."

Braddock pointed at the coffin. "Who's this one for, anyway?"

Richards grabbed his arm. "That's what I wanted to talk to you about."

Miller looked at Braddock. Braddock saw genuine sadness in the hard man's eyes.

"Doc Anderson," Miller said.

Braddock reeled back on his heels. "Anderson?" His mouth gaped open and his fists clenched. "Who could have done a thing like that? Even outlaws and killers don't shoot doctors. Everybody needs doctors."

"It was that gunfighter, Wes Carter," Richards said.

Braddock looked at him in astonishment. "But Wes is flat in bed with a fever and an arm missing."

"He's out and about now," Miller told him. He knelt down by the unfinished coffin and positioned the new board. He reached for his hammer and a nail.

"But why would Wes kill the doctor? Anderson probably saved his life."

"Richards here says Wes was sore at the doc for cutting off his arm."

Braddock looked at Richards. "How do you know that?"

"I saw him," Richards said. "Or, rather, I heard him."

"What do you mean?" Braddock was impatient.

"Doc came to find me after suppertime. It was already dark, but I was working at the bank late. He found me just coming out. But as soon as he started to talk, I heard Wes call out from the shadows, something about paying for his arm. Then a single shot and John was dead."

Braddock's jaw tightened. "I can understand his being sore about the arm, but why didn't he come after me instead?"

Richards shrugged. "You just busted it. The doc cut it off."

Miller looked up at Braddock. "And maybe he's after you too. Nobody's found him yet."

"That's right," Richards said. "That's what I wanted to talk to you about. You've got to help us find him, to make him pay for killing John Anderson, and before he finds you."

Braddock stood there seething. Then his shoulders

slumped. "No, I'm getting out of town. Tonight. Now."

Richards grabbed his arm. "But—"

Miller stopped hammering and looked up at him. "I had more respect for you than that. Guess I was wrong." He went back to hammering.

Braddock broke away from Richards' grasp. "This isn't my fight," he said angrily. "I've had my fill of this town. And what Wes might do tonight is going to seem tame compared to what Davis and McIntyre are going to do to each other tomorrow. You're going to need a barn-ful of coffins." He started leading Nick out of the barn. "By morning I can be well out of this valley."

Richards followed him. "Wes wouldn't be too hard to find. We could find him by morning."

Braddock looked at Richards and was surprised at how distressed the man seemed, as if he were more worried than angry. "No," Braddock said. He started to mount.

Miller stopped hammering again. He stood up and walked out into the patch of light as Braddock was drawing in the reins.

"Ain't you even going to pay your respects to Miss Sally?" Miller asked angrily. "She's hit hard by this. And besides, she's gonna be mighty sorry to see you leavin', anyway, if I read her right."

Braddock sagged. Of course. How could he have been so callous? And how could he have been ready to leave without seeing her pretty face just one more time?

"You're absolutely right," he said. "I need to pay my respects to Miss Anderson. Thanks for reminding me."

Miller just snorted and went back to his coffin-building.

"She's in the doctor's office," Richards said. "Some other women are helping her prepare the body."

Braddock nodded. It would be like her to do the work herself. A strong woman, a good woman. He dismounted and walked Nick toward the doctor's office. He wanted some time to think before he got there.

"I'll go with you," Richards said.

Braddock glanced at the banker but said nothing. They didn't speak all the way to the doctor's office. Braddock hitched Nick to one of the posts outside.

There were several men standing around. They were almost all wearing suits and carrying rifles or pistols. "Glad you're back, Marshal," one of them said.

"He's not marshal anymore," Richards told the man.

"What? But we need you, Braddock," the man insisted.

Braddock didn't answer. Richards said, "He's leaving Green Valley right away."

"Afraid of a one-armed man, Braddock?"

Braddock glared at the man who had spoken. "I'm not afraid of men with even two arms, mister."

The man paled. "I—I—"

"Just shut up," Braddock said.

"Yes, sir."

Braddock entered the office. Richards muttered "Stupid" to the man as he passed him, and followed Braddock inside.

In the middle of the office, Sally was talking softly with two other women while she dabbed at her tears. Braddock stepped up to her and said simply, "Sally."

"Clay!" she cried. She threw out her arms and clung desperately to him.

He was taken aback. He glanced around self-consciously, and then slowly closed his arms around her. She hugged him tighter. "Sally, I'm sorry," he said.

"He was such a good man."

"Best in the valley."

"In the world," she said. She sniffled some more. "All this trouble. He knew it was crazy and that people would get hurt. But he only worried about people, people who would need his help. He never thought it would be himself."

Braddock was at a loss for words. He clenched his jaws and looked beyond Sally at the two women standing there. They were distraught too. He glanced into the operating room. There, on the table, lay Dr. Anderson's body.

He slid his arms back so he could gently grasp Sally's arms in his hands. "I want to say good-bye to him," he said.

Sally nodded.

Richards was sure that Sally had misunderstood

Braddock's comment, and he informed her, "Braddock is leaving town right away."

"Leaving?" Her eyes searched Braddock's, and her tears increased. "Why? Why?"

He felt awful. "There's trouble coming, Sally, and it's not my trouble. It's not my fight. It's a stupid war in which a lot of people are going to get killed. Stupid and wasteful. And I don't want my life wasted."

Sally looked down at his vest. "The badge?" She stared into his eyes. "You're not marshal anymore?"

"Sally—"

Now she actually smiled and chuckled, not in humor but in irony. "My father said you were the only man in town with the slightest bit of sense."

Braddock opened his mouth, but no words came out.

She reached up and put her fingers on his lips. "Don't say anything, Clay. It's all right." As he stood there frozen, she took his hand. "Come, take a look at Father."

He nodded and let her lead him into the other room.

Dr. Anderson's corpse was dressed in a suit with a clean shirt. His hands were folded over his chest. There was no sign of the wound. Braddock squeezed Sally's hand. "I'm sorry."

"Josh is bringing a coffin."

"Yes, I know, I saw him building it."

"Funny. The last word he said to me was your name."

Braddock frowned. "How's that?"

"When he left, he said he was going to look for

Richards and you. He said, 'I have to talk to Richards and Braddock.' That's the last thing he said to me.''

"He was looking for me?'' Braddock glanced back at Richards.

Richards shrugged. "He didn't tell me he was looking for you.''

Braddock turned back to Sally. "Why did he want to see me?''

"He said Wes had been talking in his fever. He thought it was important, something about Earl Davis getting killed and how the war between Davis and McIntyre might be a mistake.''

Braddock frowned. "Something about the way Earl Davis was murdered? Richards says Doug McIntyre killed him.'' He looked at Richards again.

Richards nodded. "I was with Earl when he was killed. Or right before he was killed.''

Braddock let go of Sally's hand and walked over to Richards. "Tell me exactly what happened.''

"It was out on the north of the Davis spread, near the dry creek they call the Little Sage.''

"What were you doing out there?'' Braddock had a hard time picturing the banker riding out to backcountry, particularly in this heat.

"Davis was trying to get another loan. The bank had turned him down.''

"The bank meaning you?''

"Well, sure. Look, the place has already been mortgaged completely. There's just nothing left for collateral. But Earl wanted to show me some more country, to try to convince me that there was still more equity in the place.''

"Never mind that," Braddock said with a wave of his hand. "What about Earl's getting killed?''

"We were sitting there on our horses when somebody opened fire from the rocks ahead of us. And then this cowpoke of Davis's who was with us started shooting at us too! Earl fired back, but he was no match for two of them.''

"What were you doing all this time?" Braddock asked in irritation.

Richards took a step back. "I didn't have a gun," he said defensively. "So I took off at the first shot. I'm lucky to be alive.''

Braddock had to agree that that had been a sensible move on Richards' part. "But Davis says you saw Doug McIntyre in the rocks. Are you sure it was him?''

"Well, Douglas has this distinctive hat, you see, with those two silver conchos.''

"A hat?" Braddock asked. "You mean all you saw of the man in the rocks was his hat?''

"Well, no one else around here has a hat even remotely like that.'' Richards was sounding rather plaintive now.

Braddock frowned and stepped closer. "But maybe that's what Dr. Anderson was talking about, that you were wrong about the hat. Why, it could have been two of Davis's own men instead of only one. Maybe they just made it look like Doug McIntyre.''

"Why would Davis's own men kill Earl?" Richards said. "But the McIntyres hate the Davises."

"But maybe it wasn't Doug McIntyre. What happened to the cowhand, Willard Pyle? Where did you see him go?"

Richards shrugged. "I didn't look back. Nobody's seen Pyle since. Wouldn't *you* disappear?"

Braddock had to admit to himself that that was sensible too.

Sally stepped over to his side. "What are you thinking, Clay?"

He shrugged helplessly. "No matter. It's probably too late, anyway. Wish your father had found me, though. Or, at least, had a chance to talk to Richards here."

Richards looked contrite. "What could *I* do?"

Braddock turned to Sally. "Sally, I. . . ." He looked at her beautiful face. What a terrible dilemma. Leave or stay? If he stayed, he could be dead in a day. If he left, he would always be tortured by what might have been.

He looked beyond her in desperation, not being able to keep looking into those eyes. He was startled. The other room, the one they used as a tiny hospital, was a shambles. "What happened in there?" he asked, frowning.

She followed his glance. "Wes must have gone berserk. The place was wrecked when I got back from the jail."

"The jail?"

"Yes. I was taking food over to your prisoner. But he was gone."

"Gone! Someone let Milo out?"

"The cell door was open and the keys were lying on the desk."

Braddock was now sure he had to leave town.

"And when I got back here," Sally went on, "I found the room looking like this, and Wes was gone too. Why, I'm surprised he could even walk."

"He must have been desperate, and desperate men do desperate things."

"And you know, the shot I heard on the way back here must have been the shot that killed Father."

Braddock touched her cheek. "I'm so sorry."

She nodded and smiled lamely.

"Sally." He stared at her, still torn. Then he looked at Richards and at the two women in the other room, who were both staring at him, and at two other men who had come into that room. "Sally, could I talk to you outside?"

She looked puzzled. "All right, Clay."

They walked out into the night and stopped near Nick. "Sally, I've done some dumb things in my life, and I think I'm about to do another one by leaving Green Valley and you."

Sally smiled warmly. "Thank you for saying that, Clay. I will miss you too. We just met, but already I. . . ."

Braddock nodded. "I know, I know." He sighed.

"I understand," she murmured. "I truly do."

"Can you forgive me for leaving? Or ever have a kind thought about me again?"

She reached up and gently touched the stitches on his wound. "I shall always think only kind thoughts about you."

He laid his hand on hers. "Sally—"

But he was interrupted by gunfire down the street. He looked in that direction, but could see nothing amiss on the dark street. Lights shone in a few windows and from the livery stable. "That was a shotgun," he said.

"Probably Father's," Sally told him. "That must be Wes shooting. He took Father's shotgun."

Braddock shuddered. Wes had killed the doctor with a shotgun. And Sally had prepared him for burial with that awful wound! He felt greater agony over the woman's sorrow, and greater admiration for her courage and strength.

"Someone's coming," a man said.

Braddock looked down the street. Running towards them was Josh Miller.

He was panting heavily by the time he reached the doctor's office. "It's Wes," he gasped. "Blew a hole in the coffin I was working on and then tried to kill me. But I was out the door already."

"What's he after you for?" Braddock asked. "You didn't have anything to do with his arm."

"He's taking a horse and leavin' town."

Braddock turned to the men standing near the office. "Well, go get him!" he shouted.

The men fidgeted. "That Wes is loco," someone

said. "You ever see what a scattergun will do to a man?"

"There's five of you."

"One shotgun is enough for me," the answer came.

Braddock was fuming now. He reached for Nick's saddle and touched the familiar leather. In a minute he could be out of town and away from Wes's shotgun, and away from Milo, and away from all the trouble.

In growing anger Miller looked from Sally to the men. Then he said in disgust: "Give *me* a rifle, then. That Wes killed a good friend of mine, and I ain't lettin' him leave town." He started toward the men.

Braddock straightened up. "Richards!" he bellowed.

Everyone froze, and Richards came rushing outside. "What?"

Braddock walked up to him and stuck out his hand, palm up. "Gimme the badge," he said.

Braddock pinned the tin star on his vest once again. He glared at the armed men standing around the doctor's office, but he didn't say anything. Sally stepped toward him when he moved toward his horse. "Clay," she said, and she reached out to touch his sleeve.

He yanked his Winchester from its saddle scabbard. "I'll bring him in, Sally," he promised. "He'll pay for what he did. This won't take long." He gave Sally's arm a little squeeze. "I'll be back." He set off for the livery stable with long strides.

Miller called after him, "I'm comin' with you."

Then he bellowed at the men standing idly in the shadows, "If you tadpoles ain't gonna use those Winchesters, let me have one of 'em." He yanked a carbine from the nearest man.

The man didn't complain. "That Wes is loco," he warned.

"He don't scare me!" Miller scampered after Braddock.

Braddock stopped, rested a fist on his hip, and looked at Miller. "This isn't your job."

"Butler's buttons!" Miller said, going ahead of Braddock. "This ain't even yours, really. You're just a cowhand, for a fact."

Braddock had to smile. They were both striding rapidly now. "Okay. Glad to have an extra gun backing me up. Can you shoot that thing?"

"Been using a gun since before you were as tall as a Winchester."

"Good. But I want to take Wes alive, understand? I want to find out what he told Dr. Anderson."

"Makes sense, Marshal. I figure that with only one arm, it might take him a while to saddle a horse, and maybe it'll also make him a poor shot, to boot."

"Nobody's a poor shot with a shotgun, so don't count on that."

Hearing footsteps behind them, they looked back to see Richards trotting up, a carbine in his hands.

"You too?" Braddock asked.

"John Anderson was a good friend of mine, Marshal."

"Okay, but can you handle that Winchester?"

"Sure," Richards said, and he worked the lever of the weapon while looking down at it. The muzzle of the gun waved in Braddock's face.

"Look out!" Braddock snapped. He pushed the barrel away. "Watch where you're pointing that thing."

"Oh, sorry." Richards pointed the carbine at the ground.

"Just stay behind me," Braddock said. "Better yet, stay off to one side. I'd rather not get shot in the back of the head."

Richards looked chagrined, but he said nothing. Miller motioned them both on. "Come on! Wes was in a hurry."

They headed down the street again and reached the livery stable just as Wes was leading a horse out through the front doors. He was holding both the reins and a shotgun with his one hand. He was panting heavily and swearing to himself. He wore neither a hat nor a shirt, and his chest and shoulder were wrapped in bandages. Even in the dim light, Braddock could see that Wes was sweating profusely from the fever and his work.

"Wes Carter!" he roared.

Wes spun around. He let go of the reins but not the shotgun. The horse stopped.

"Braddock, is that you?" Wes asked frantically. He squinted into the darkness. The three men approaching him had not entered the light from the open livery doors. Wes awkwardly wiped the sweat from his eyes with his bare left arm, and again he tried to pick out the figures in the dark.

"You're under arrest!" Braddock said. "Put the shotgun down." He raised his Winchester with the hammer cocked.

Wes juggled the shotgun around in his hand until he had it by the grip with his finger on the trigger. "Who's that with you?" He brought the barrel up and traversed slowly along the line of the three men.

"Look out, Marshal!" Richards cried. He snapped up his Winchester and fired a wild shot into the interior of the stable.

Wes pulled the triggers on both barrels of the shotgun. His horse leaped and whinnied at the crash and trotted off down the street.

Braddock, Richards, and Miller jumped in different directions. Richards stumbled and fell.

"Wes, put it down!" Braddock ordered. "Now! You used both barrels, and I can see you're not wearing a pistol." He looked quickly over at Richards, who was sitting up. "You hurt?"

Richards had dropped his Winchester and was holding the sleeve of his suit coat. "He shredded it, Marshal. He could have killed me." His voice was panicky.

Braddock looked back at Wes. The man had cracked open the shotgun and had it gripped between his knees. He plucked the two empty shells from the chambers and tossed them aside. Then he fished in his pocket for two new rounds. He jammed them into the shotgun's chambers and snapped the gun shut. He seized the grip and labored to get both hammers cocked with his one hand. Then he brought the shotgun up again.

"Don't be a fool, Wes!" Braddock could see that Wes was seething in anger. "I don't want to hurt you again. You told Doc Anderson something. I want to know what you told him."

But Wes was hissing hot breath through his teeth. "It's your fault I lost my arm. And then you tried to kill me." The shotgun's barrel wandered back and forth.

"I didn't fire that shot," Braddock said. "Just put the—"

The shotgun boomed again. Richards yelped. As Miller brought his Winchester up, Braddock cried, "No! Wait!"

Miller fired.

Wes staggered backward, but he straightened up. "It'll take more than that," he said. He was a tough man. The shotgun's barrel started to follow Richards, not Braddock. Richards was scrambling on his hands and knees into deeper darkness.

"Wes! I'm over here!" Braddock shouted, but Wes ignored him. Braddock fired. Wes spun around, and the shotgun fired into the night sky. The gunman twisted to the ground and slumped into stillness.

Braddock hurried over to him and knelt down. Wes was dead. Braddock sagged back on his heels. He pounded a fist on his leg. Miller and Richards came up and looked down at the dead man lying in the dim light from the livery stable.

"You got him for good this time, Marshal," Miller said.

Braddock looked up. "What could I do? Shoot his other arm off?"

"He might have killed me," Richards said. He wiped his brow even though the evening was no longer hot. "You had to do it."

"He must have mistaken you for me in the dark with the sweat in his eyes," Braddock said.

Miller shook his head. "Oh, I don't know. Nobody likes bankers, somehow."

Richards scowled at him.

Braddock stood up and angrily stepped closer to Richards. "And why'd you fire that first shot? I wanted Wes alive. He knew something."

Richards backed away. "I'm sorry, Marshal, but I thought he was going to shoot you. I was just trying to protect you."

Incompetent, Braddock thought. Then he glared at Miller. "You didn't help, either, by shooting him in the side like that."

"He fired first," Miller said. "Hooker's books, Marshal, did I have to let him shoot me?"

Braddock sighed and looked down at the dead man. He reached for the shotgun on the ground and picked it up. "Well, looks like you need yet another coffin, Josh."

Miller stepped to the body. "Marshal's expenses?" he asked softly.

Braddock just stared down at Wes, wondering what the gunman had told Dr. Anderson that made the doctor want to see the marshal. ''Marshal's expenses,'' he said disgustedly.

Chapter Seven

The men had left the doctor's office by the time Braddock returned there, but the two women were still with Sally sitting quietly on chairs in the front office. Sally was in her father's big office chair, arms on the rests, eyes staring blankly ahead, rocking slowly.

Braddock entered with her father's shotgun. "Wes is dead," he announced. "I had to shoot him."

"He killed the doctor," one of the two visiting women said. "He deserved to die."

"That's so," Braddock agreed reluctantly.

Sally came alert and looked up at him. "Did you find out what my father wanted to see you about?"

"Didn't have a chance. That fool Richards took a shot at Wes before I had a chance to talk with him. Wes naturally shot back, and I had to shoot him."

Sally slumped back down again. "Oh." She started to rock slowly.

Braddock rested the shotgun against the wall. "Here's your father's shotgun. I'm not sure you want it anymore."

"Just leave it there."

The two other women rose, and one of them said,

"Sally, we need to be going, but we'll be back early in the morning."

"Thank you."

"Sure you don't want to stay with one of us tonight, instead of here alone with your father?"

Sally smiled bleakly. "I want to be together with him, not alone with him. I'd like to spend one last night in our home together. But thank you for asking."

The woman nodded. "We understand. And don't worry about fixing anything for after the burial tomorrow afternoon. We'll take care of everything."

"Tomorrow afternoon?" Braddock repeated.

Sally nodded. "We've sent for the Reverend Merriman from over in Johnson's Flats. He should get here by late tomorrow afternoon. We thought sunset would be a proper time for interment."

He nodded. In this heat it wouldn't do to have the good doctor's body waiting for days.

The women started through the door. "Good night, Marshal," they said together.

"Good night, ladies."

"Thank you for killing that gunfighter," one of them said.

"Clay?" Sally said when they were alone. "You're not pleased with having killed Wes, are you?"

He sat down on a straight chair, took off his hat, and wiped his brow. He rested his elbows on his knees and leaned forward. Idly he let the hat dangle in front of him, holding it by the very edge of the brim. "Sally, I've killed three men since sunset."

"My father liked you, Clay Braddock."

"He hardly knew me."

"He was very good at making quick and accurate judgments about people, and he said he could tell you were a good man. Tough when you had to be, but no tougher than was needed. A good, sensible, valuable man."

Braddock smiled in embarrassment.

"Did you ever kill a man before this?"

He sat back in the chair and rested his hat on his lap. "I've won more fistfights than I've lost. I shot a couple of men who needed doctoring bad after it. But I killed only one man before this. He was with a pack of rustlers who tried to take our herd one night in the middle of a rainstorm. A couple of thousand steers trampled him before we got to his body. His face was gone. Could hardly tell it was a man, in fact. So it was sort of like I hadn't killed a man, not a real man. But these three were men I'd met before, and knew their faces."

"They certainly weren't friends of yours," Sally said. "Hired gunmen, all three. Killed other men themselves, no doubt."

Braddock nodded. "I don't say I did anything wrong. Just can't see what's so important that requires all this killing going on."

Sally smiled again. "Just like my father felt. And me too. Clay, I wish there was something I could do to stop all of this. My father never found the solution."

"I thought of maybe giving it one more try, of going

out to see Davis tomorrow early. Maybe I could get him to listen to me. He might like a way out too, if he could see one.''

''Did McIntyre listen yesterday?''

''No,'' Braddock admitted. ''And I don't suppose I'll have much luck with Davis, either, but maybe it's worth the chance. I'd like to try for your father's sake.''

''I'd like that.''

''In fact, maybe you could help.''

''How?'' She stopped rocking.

''Well, what if we went out to Davis together? See, if I go out there alone, he might just toss me out on my ear, badge or no badge. But I've got a feeling that you'd be treated with a lot more respect.''

A smile grew slowly on Sally's face. ''My father said you were clever too. So, you think it would go like this: My father having been the most respected man in the valley, you figure that his daughter in mourning for him would naturally get a careful hearing from Davis. And from McIntyre too, for that matter.''

Braddock nodded. ''What do you think? We might make a pretty good team. Where I come from, two heads can make more sense than one.''

''Let's try,'' Sally said. ''Tomorrow early.''

''Good. Tomorrow early.'' And then he just smiled at her.

The next day Braddock realized that he had been right about bringing Sally. Whereas, two miles from the Davis ranch compound, the guards had glowered at him on his horse, they had shown the utmost courtesy and respect upon seeing that it was Sally Anderson in the buggy that was accompanying him. They paid her the kind of attention that only lonely cowhands can show to a ministering angel they had long worshiped from afar.

When Braddock and Sally were ushered into the immense living room of the main house, Davis himself was genuinely and profusely sympathetic and respectful. And it was clear that he not only had held John Anderson in the highest regard, but he had deep admiration for Sally in her own right too.

Harlan and Randy hovered around Sally as well, but Braddock could easily tell that it was more than sympathy that motivated the two young men. After the greetings and formalities, Sally said, "Mr. Davis, the funeral for my father is late this afternoon, depending on when Reverend Merriman gets here from Johnson's Flats."

"Miss Sally, you can be sure we'll all be there."

"Even if the McIntyres are there too, Sally," Randy chimed in, trying to sound cheerful.

His father glared at him. "That's a stupid thing to say at a time like this."

"Pa," Harlan said, "Randy was just trying to tell Sally that nothing would keep us away. He meant no harm."

Sally smiled politely at the young men. "Thank you, Randy, Harlan. I'd appreciate your both being there."

Davis took Sally's hand, squeezed it, and smiled.

"Miss Sally, you know I always told your father I'd trade any two of my boys for you. I envied him his daughter."

Sally smiled. "He told me many times, sir."

"Kind of hoped that Earl might get you here in another way."

Braddock's face flushed at that thought, but he realized that Sally had to be the most sought-after young woman in the valley.

Randy edged closer to her. "With Earl gone, Sally, maybe Harlan and me have a chance to—"

His father dropped Sally's hand and cracked Randy across the face with the back of his own hand, so hard that Randy spun around and stumbled into a chair. Then Davis cried, "How can you say a thing like that with your brother fresh in his grave!" A massive fist was pulling back, and Randy was cowering on the chair.

"Pa, I'm sorry," Randy said. "Please don't hit me."

Braddock felt unsure of himself. It was none of his business, to be sure. Still, this didn't seem right to him. He noticed that Harlan didn't move a muscle.

When Harlan saw Braddock look at him, he merely muttered, "This time I'm not gonna try to help the idiot."

It was Sally who caught Davis's uplifted arm. "Please, Mr. Davis."

Davis looked at her, and his arm came down slowly. "I'm sorry," he said and backed away.

Randy collapsed onto the floor in relief. He scooted

a few feet away and rose quickly to stand quietly off to the side.

"Fool son," Davis muttered. "Sagebrush has got more brains than he has."

Braddock looked over at Randy, and he thought Davis might just as well have punched him with the fist as say something like that about him, particularly in front of Sally. Not that Randy's remark hadn't been as stupid as his father had said.

"Well, Mr. Davis," Sally said, "his father is not acting any too smart himself right now."

"What?" Davis straightened up, startled. He clenched his jaw. "Miss Sally, those are strong words. If you were a man—"

"That's the trouble," she told him. "All you can think of doing is striking out."

"I think," Davis said sternly, "that how I handle my sons is *my* business."

"I wasn't talking about your sons. I'm talking about this valley, and the drought, and McIntyre, and—"

"Don't talk to me about the McIntyres!" Davis shouted.

Sally pressed on: "I'm sure the McIntyres will indeed be at the funeral. What's going to happen when you get there?"

Davis fumed a little, and then settled down. "In respect for you and your father, there will be no trouble."

"And after that?"

"Doug McIntyre put my son in the ground, and I'm

going to hang him for it.'' He glanced over at Braddock. ''Unless the law will do it for me. You'd like that better, wouldn't you, Marshal?'' There was contempt in the address.

''What if Doug didn't do it?'' Sally said. ''It could have been someone else. Why don't you look for Willard Pyle?''

''I don't need any more talk!'' Davis thundered. He stalked away and pounded a fist on a table. A lamp bounced and rattled. ''This valley's no longer big enough for both us and the McIntyres.''

Braddock stepped forward. ''Not at the moment it isn't, Mr. Davis,'' he said. ''But it's just this drought. And that'll pass sooner or later. It always does.''

Davis stalked up to Braddock. ''If you hadn't come with Miss Sally, I'd put another gash on your other cheek, just to give her something else to sew.''

Braddock stood his ground. ''You've got too many cows on the range. You ought to slaughter most of them.''

''There's no market for 'em. It'd be a complete loss. I can't afford that. Besides, if I cut back on my herds, McIntyre would simply let his cows take over the range.''

''But that's the same thing that McIntyre says about you,'' Braddock said in exasperation.

Harlan jumped in now. ''We aren't talking about cattle anyway. It's the McIntyres themselves.''

''That's right,'' Davis agreed. ''And when they're

gone, the cows won't matter. There'll just be Davis cows.''

"But you can't be sure it was Doug McIntyre who killed Earl," Braddock said.

"Richards saw him." Davis waved his hand. "That's that."

"All Richards saw was a hat like Doug's. Maybe he saw the hat because he was expecting to see the hat, or because someone wanted him to see it. I'm not impressed by Richards' ability to see anything straight.''

Davis snorted. "Well, he's got a keen eye for a dollar, the leech.''

"Richards says the bank is squeezing you pretty tight," Braddock said with a frown. "But it's your bank too, isn't it?''

Davis snorted again, and stalked away.

"*Used* to be Pa's bank," Harlan said. "He was a founder and a major stockholder.''

Braddock peered at Harlan. "What happened?''

"The drought. We've had tremendous losses. He had to sell out to Richards, Bennett, and Taylor last year in order to raise cash. Lost his seat on the board too. They let Earl stay on the board, but just for looks. And Earl never got along with Richards and the others.''

"How come it was Earl who was trying to get Richards to give you another loan just before he was killed?''

"Was he?''

"Isn't that why Richards and your brother went out to look at that land?" Braddock asked.

Harlan shrugged. "I thought Richards had asked to meet Earl. Whatever the exact reason, it doesn't matter. Doug McIntyre saw to that, him and that weasel, Willard Pyle. Worked for us for twelve years, he did. Then he does something like this. For a little money."

"And no one's seen him since?"

"Nope."

Davis stalked up. "Enough jabbering. I can't stand hearing about it. The McIntyres go, and that's that."

Braddock held up a hand. "But what if it wasn't Doug? He claims he's got a dozen men who will swear he was at the McIntyre ranch at the time."

"Probably two dozen, if he wants them," Davis said. "What would you expect his own men to say?"

"I'd like to see the spot where Earl was killed."

"What for?"

"I'm not sure. I'm just not convinced that Doug McIntyre did it."

"Too late," Harlan said.

"Why?" Braddock asked.

"Shut up, Harlan," Davis ordered.

Braddock looked at Davis. "What's going on?"

"Why don't you take Miss Sally back to town, Marshal?" Davis said.

Sally stepped closer to Davis again. "Not until you agree to talk to Angus McIntyre. Mr. Davis, you and Angus McIntyre must talk to each other. Even if Douglas did kill Earl. This valley is about to run with blood. You just have to talk to each other.''

"McIntyre wouldn't talk to me,'' Davis said. "And I've got nothing to talk to him about.''

Sally held up a single finger. "Just once,'' she urged. After the funeral. You and McIntyre in my father's office.'' She put a hand on Davis's arm. "For my father's sake and for Earl's. The killing has to stop.''

Davis looked down at Sally, and Braddock could see him melting. "All right, Miss Sally,'' he murmured. "For you.'' His voice had softened. He shook his head slowly. "But McIntyre doesn't want to talk to me any more than I want to talk to him.''

"Let me try to persuade him,'' Sally said. "I'll go over there right now.''

"I'd better go with you,'' Braddock said.

"No!'' Davis cried.

Braddock looked sideways at Davis. "Why not?''

"Because—'' Davis paused. "Because Harlan's going to show you where Earl was killed.''

"I am?'' Harlan said in surprise.

Randy took a tentative step forward. "I'll go with Sally to the McIntyres','' he suggested cheerily.

"And get your head blown off?'' Davis said sharply. "Use what little brains you got. Go with Harlan and show Braddock where your brother died.''

"Yes, sir.''

"Move!'' Davis ordered. Both his sons moved quickly. Davis turned to Sally. "You're the only one who could get me talk to McIntyre before Earl's killer has been brought to justice." He patted her gently on the shoulder. "If there's anything you need. . . ."

"I know. Thank you."

Braddock and Sally left the ranch house and walked to the buggy.

"That Davis is a hard man," Braddock said. "Bullheaded. No wonder nothing can get settled peacefully."

Sally mounted the seat with an assisting hand from Braddock. "Is McIntyre any different?"

"No. Where I come from, men have to be like that to settle a country. Guess it's the same up here. He doesn't have to take it out on his sons, though."

Sally picked up the reins. "He drives them hard, but he wants them able to run the ranch when he's gone."

"I think Harlan will run the ranch without any regard for Randy. I doubt Randy's father wants him to have anything to do with running the ranch."

"Luckily, Harlan will watch out for him. He's very protective of his little brother."

Braddock gathered Nick's reins from the hitching rail. "Is it true about you and Earl?"

"Earl did come calling. So did others." She smiled a little. "Jealous?"

"Me? No, 'course not." He mounted Nick and led him a few steps so that he was even with Sally in her buggy. "Well, yes, I guess I am."

Sally laughed. "Good-bye, Clay. I'll see you back in town after I get back from McIntyre's place."

"Okay. I don't need to go with you to McIntyre's. You're the one who tamed Davis."

"It was your suggestion that I come. I guess we do make a good team, like you say."

She waved a hand and flicked the reins. The buggy moved off. Braddock watched her pull away and head out of the compound yard. Harlan and Randy joined him on horseback.

"Mighty fine woman there," Harlan commented.

"None that fine where I come from," Braddock said.

"Earl didn't have her cut out," Randy said, peeved.

"That's true," Harlan agreed. "She just didn't seem interested in being roped by any of us. But she's real sweet about it. Could tell you to go jump off a cliff and make you eager to do it for her."

"I can believe that," Braddock said.

It was a long northeast ride away from the main Davis ranch compound. The sun was almost at high, and the day was another scorcher. Harlan and Randy led Braddock to the Little Sage Creek, the spot where Earl had been gunned down. It was a dry creekbed in a small depression.

"Been no water in it for two years now," Harlan said. "Even in spring."

Behind them to the south and to the west stretched open desert. To the northeast was a rock outcropping about twenty feet high. There was a jumble of rocks between the outcropping and the riders, and they could have gone no farther on horseback. It was a hundred yards at least.

To the north about half a mile away was a cliff face, again with a jumble of rocks along the foot. Although not particularly high, the cliff showed no obvious means of passage to the top.

Harlan pointed to the ground ahead of them. "Found Earl's body lying right there."

"Richards said Doug McIntyre fired at them from the rocks to the northeast, ahead of us," Braddock said.

"That's what Richards said," Harlan confirmed.

Braddock looked around at the desert and the rocks. "You know, this doesn't look like a likely spot for an ambush. Earl was still pretty much in the open, far away from those rocks up ahead."

"It's within easy Winchester range."

"But how did the ambusher know that Earl would come to this spot? There's no road that leads this way and no reason to come to this very spot."

"Maybe it was Willard's job to lead them here," Harlan said. "Or Doug just followed them. When Earl and Richards stopped here and got to talking, Doug went around and up ahead and got into the rocks. No reason this spot had to have been selected ahead of time."

Braddock nodded slowly. "That could be . . . yes." He twisted in the saddle and looked back. "It's just flat country behind us. How come Earl didn't notice someone following them?"

"Earl wasn't expecting to be followed. He had no reason to be looking back."

"How come you suppose Richards got away?" Braddock asked.

"Ran like a rabbit?" Randy suggested.

"Maybe they wanted him to get away," Braddock said.

Harlan stared at him. "Why?"

"To make sure everyone would think it was Doug McIntyre when it wasn't."

Harlan considered that, and then shook his head. "No, Doug wants everybody to know he did it. Then he gets a dozen of his men to say he couldn't have done it, so he can't be hanged for doing it."

"There's some sense to that," Braddock stroked his jaw.

"But we're not going to let him get away with it," Randy said. "If the law won't hang Doug, we will."

"Did you go after Willard?" Braddock asked.

Harlan shook his head. "By the time we got out here, hours had passed, and he was long gone."

"Were there any tracks?"

"Sure, headed straight north. He probably didn't stop till he hit Canada."

"Tell you what," Braddock said. "Randy, I'd like you to get up into those rocks ahead of us and find the empty shell casings that the ambusher left behind."

"What for?" Randy asked.

"Maybe they were an unusual caliber or something.

This whole thing just doesn't seem right to me, and I want to look at everything I can.''

"Aw, this is silly," Randy protested.

"Randy," Harlan said, "get going."

Randy kicked his horse's sides and muttered something about older brothers.

Braddock watched Randy ride hard off to the side to get around behind the rocks, which would take him a while. He looked back at Harlan. "Did Earl treat Randy the same way you do?"

"Keep him busy—that's the important thing. What do we do while he hunts?"

Braddock nodded toward the north. "Let's take a look at the cliff, about where those two buzzards are circling.''

"What for?"

"Where I come from, sometimes you have to search before you know what you're looking for.'' Braddock gave Nick a nudge, and the horse started walking northward.

"You're just wasting time, Braddock. I think you need to go back to where you're from."

"Sooner I get out of this place, the better I'll like it. And if you help me, I'll be gone sooner than if you don't.''

Harlan snorted. "Good point." He spurred his horse.

The two men rode toward the cliff. It was not a long ride, but it got increasingly more difficult as the land came in a series of rises and jumbled rocks. They stopped when they reached a dead horse, still saddled, lying in a gully.

"No wonder there are buzzards still hanging around," Braddock said, looking down.

Harlan nodded. "That horse has been here a long time. The coyotes and vultures have picked him over pretty good."

"Don't you think it's odd that the horse is still saddled?" Braddock asked. He had to nudge Nick twice to get him to move toward the carcass. They descended the gully slope and stopped a few feet from the animal's remains. "Who would leave a saddle behind?" Braddock asked Harlan. "That doesn't make sense."

Harlan guided his horse down into the gully. He circled the carcass, studied the saddle, then looked up at Braddock. His face showed surprise as he said, "This is Willard Pyle's horse."

The two men stared at each other a moment. "Still think he's in Canada?" Braddock asked.

Harlan ran a hand over his chin. "Well. . . ."

"Assuming that Willard's horse was shot from under him, where would he have gone? I'd say to high ground. Up there." Braddock pointed to a likely spot.

He dismounted and led Nick on foot now. They went up out of the gully and headed up a slope. Harlan also dismounted and followed, leading his horse.

Braddock soon found a pistol in the sand, and he was checking the cylinder as Harlan came abreast. "Six empty cartridges." He handed it to Harlan. "Willard's?"

Harlan shrugged. "Wouldn't know."

Braddock dropped the pistol and led Nick farther up the slope to the crest. On the other side he looked down and saw the remains of a man lying near the cliff face. The bones had been scattered by the scavengers of the night and day, but clothes still clung to parts of the tooth-cleaned skeleton. Harlan joined Braddock and looked down at the carcass.

"Willard?" Braddock asked.

"Can't tell for sure from up here."

So they went down and circled the corpse.

"Look at his gun belt," Braddock said. "Not a single cartridge left."

"It's Willard's clothes and Willard's horse. It has to be him."

Braddock took off his hat and wiped his brow. "I hate having to think this hard." He put his hat back on. "Why was Willard killed? It doesn't make any sense."

"The killer didn't want a witness."

"But you just said Doug McIntyre would have wanted people to know he'd done it."

"But not be able to prove it," Harlan countered.

"But what about Richards? He was a witness, and the killer didn't hunt him down and kill him. Just look at Willard. I'd say he put up quite a fight. Not a cartridge left."

"I just don't know."

"Willard was a partner, not a victim. Not at first. Willard helped someone murder Earl and make Richards think it was Doug. And then the killer made sure Willard would never be able to tell who the real killer was.''

Harlan's brow was furrowed. He rubbed a hand nervously on his trousers. Then he shook his head slowly. ''Braddock, what you say makes—''

Just then, a rifle bullet twanged off the rocks near Braddock's head.

Chapter Eight

Braddock and Harlan both snatched Winchesters from saddle scabbards. Then they hustled to cover behind separate rocks as several more shots kicked at their heels. The two horses trotted back down the way they had come.

"You see him?" Harlan called from behind his rock.

"Over on the left somewhere, I think," Braddock said.

"Big help that is." Harlan peered over the rock. Nothing happened. He ducked back down. "Must be Doug McIntyre. Or maybe that fat man Milo and some of his boys."

"Only seems to be one man. And how can you be sure it's Doug or Milo? We haven't seen anything yet."

"Who else would it be?" Harlan answered.

"That's what Richards said about the hat, isn't it?"

"Bah. You're trying too hard." Harlan looked over the rock again. "No more shots. Suppose he's gone already?"

"There are two of us and only one of him. It would be sensible for him not to press the attack once he's lost the element of surprise." As Braddock peered over his rock, a bullet thwacked into it. He ducked back down. "Nope, not gone. Maybe he's just moving across in front of us."

The two men were quiet. A minute passed, then another. Braddock peered cautiously over his rock. He saw a hat and then a rifle barrel. "There!" He fired and got a fusillade of bullets for an answer.

"Must be half a dozen of them now!" Harlan cried. He was firing rapidly.

"Don't waste your shots."

"Got one of 'em!" Harlan shouted.

Braddock fired once more, and then the firing stopped. He looked over at Harlan. "See any?"

Harlan shook his head.

A voice called from behind the rocks. "Braddock!"

Braddock slumped against the rock. "Milo," he said in disgust.

"See, I told you it was McIntyre's men," Harlan declared triumphantly.

Braddock had to admit that Harlan had been right. "What do you want?" he called out to Milo.

"Seems you're in a bad spot. Not only are you stuck there, but you just shot two of my men. Now I'm really mad. And there's still five of us left."

"You don't care about your men." Braddock looked both ways. There was no back entrance in the cliff face.

"And you got Harlan Davis with you," Milo yelled. "Bad luck. We're lookin' for him."

Harlan nodded slowly. He looked angrily at Braddock. "First Earl, then me. Still got any doubts, Braddock?"

Maybe not, Braddock thought. This was no accidental meeting. "We have to make it to the horses, Harlan," he said. "Can you see them?"

Harlan nodded. "A long way off and still moving. If you cover me, I'll make a run for them. Then I'll cover you."

Braddock realized that making a run for the horses would make good targets of them, but there was no point in trying to wait out Milo and his men. "Go!"

Harlan broke from cover. Braddock snapped up his Winchester and fired once, but he had no target at first. And then he had lots of targets. He fired rapidly and so did his attackers. Bullets twanged off the rocks around him. Then Harlan screamed.

Braddock dropped out of sight and looked over to his left. Harlan had fallen and slid to a stop. He had dropped his carbine too. Finally Harlan started moving again, slowly. He crawled behind a rock.

The firing tapered off. Milo shouted again. "We hit Harlan. Is he dead yet?"

Harlan did his own answering. He drew his pistol and fired blindly over the rock. "Not yet!" Then he pulled the bandanna from around his neck and started stuffing it into a wound in his side.

Milo laughed. "Well, won't be long. Where'd that other brother go, the fellow you rode out here with?"

Harlan and Braddock looked at each other. "Good question," Braddock muttered to himself.

But Randy answered. "Right behind you!"

There was a quick three or four shots from Randy's carbine, a stream of cursing from Milo and his men, and someone yelped.

Braddock looked up over the rock. Randy's head and arm and carbine could be seen above the rocks directly behind Milo and his men.

They were caught in between. One of Milo's men threw himself against a rock for protection against Randy's fire, but he was then in plain view of Braddock and he realized it immediately. Braddock raised his carbine. The man leaped up to run back to the first rock, but he got only a few feet before Braddock's bullet knocked him back into the second rock.

Milo was shouting. No more shots came. Randy fired again and then started hurrahing and laughing. "Run, run, run!"

Braddock heard hoofbeats again. They faded quickly. Randy sauntered down from the rocks, leading his horse.

Braddock went over to Harlan, lying in the sand behind his rock. He was breathing rapidly and clenching his teeth in pain. After a look at the wound, Braddock settled back on his heels. "I don't think it's real serious," he said.

"Well, it still hurts!" Harlan snapped. As Randy came up, Harlan glared at him. "And where were you when all the shooting was going on?"

"I thought it was you two at first," Randy said with a shrug.

"If you'd come right away, maybe I wouldn't have this bullet in my side."

"I still had to sneak up behind them. That took time."

"No matter," Braddock said. "We have to get your brother back to town to—" He didn't finish.

"Doc's dead, remember?" Randy said. "We'll just let Pa carve the bullet out."

Harlan flinched. He closed his eyes and shook his head. "I don't want Pa to do any carving on me."

"Sally could take that out, I'll bet," Braddock said.

"A woman?" Randy asked. He laughed.

"She put the stitches in my cheek."

Harlan looked at the neatly stitched wound. Then he nodded. "Okay. Get me to Sally."

"She's over at McIntyre's at the moment," Braddock reminded him.

"Well, we sure can't go over there."

"We'll take you to town, and I'll bring her there as quick as I can." Braddock stood up. "Randy, you have to catch our horses."

"I already did," Randy informed him. "They're way back."

Harlan snapped his head around. "Thought you said you came as quick as you could once you knew it wasn't us doing all the shooting. How come you had time to catch those horses?"

"I was looking for shell casings, remember?" Randy turned his back and started to walk away, leading his horse.

"Let me see them," Braddock said.

"Didn't find any."

"No shell casings? That's odd."

Randy spun around. "You gonna say I didn't look?" he snapped. "Say I couldn't find my head if it wasn't attached to my body? Well, go look yourself. I looked plenty." He mounted his horse, gave it a savage kick, and surged away.

"Who would bother picking up shell casings after an ambush?" Braddock mused aloud.

"Aw, Randy can't even find his boots in the morning. It was a dumb idea to be looking for shell casings, anyway. No point to it. Hope Milo convinced you of that."

Braddock ignored the implied insult. Randy disappeared over the rise now.

"Harlan, did you get the feeling that the man shooting at us at first wasn't the same man as the one who shot at us next? I mean the shots came from two completely different directions."

Harlan squinted at Braddock. "Milo probably just crossed over behind the rocks in front of us. Then he waited till his men caught up to him. What are you getting at?"

"How well did your brothers get along with each other?"

"What?" Harlan painfully knocked himself against the rock with his outburst. Then he sat up slowly, grimacing. "You're loco, Braddock. All three of us fought like cougars, but we're brothers first. If anybody in the family was going to get shot, it would've been Pa.''

''It would explain why Willard was killed, though. And Willard would have been more easily enlisted by Randy than by Doug McIntyre.''

Harlan picked up a handful of sand and threw it feebly at Braddock's boot. ''You've had too much sun and too much locoweed. If I didn't have this bullet in me, I'd get up and pound you flat for what you're thinking.''

''But this all has to make sense,'' Braddock insisted. ''Why pounce on us just when we'd found Willard?''

''Are you gonna say next that Randy just brought in Milo and his bunch? Or why didn't he just let Milo finish us off if he didn't want us to know about Willard?''

Braddock nodded slowly. ''That does figure. But what if Randy had been the one shooting at us at first, and Milo had simply heard the shots and come over to investigate. Randy would have backed off when he'd seen Milo coming, and Milo would have seen who we were and taken up the ambush himself.''

Harlan shook his head. ''It's all just coincidence. You heard what Milo said. No. Milo and his men were hunting for us. They were sent out to get us.'' He laughed sardonically. ''Seems fair, I guess.''

Braddock frowned and looked down at Harlan. ''What do you mean?''

''Nothin', I don't mean nothin'.''

Braddock's scalp twinged.

* * *

Braddock soon had Nick going at a fast canter toward the McIntyre ranch, located cross-country from the Little Sage ambush. He knew that Harlan needed help quickly, but he didn't want to wear down Nick in the blistering heat. And Randy would have to go slowly with Harlan to minimize the bleeding on the way to the doctor's office in town. Braddock thought he might be able to find Sally and get her back to town not too long after Randy and Harlan arrived there.

He pulled Nick up, stopped his pondering, and studied the dust plume racing along the McIntyre road off to his far right. It looked like a buggy going as fast as its driver could force the horse, a dangerous practice in this heat.

That could be Sally's buggy, going back to town from McIntyre's. Had she lost control? Was something wrong? He gave Nick a kick and sent him off on a run. "Sorry about this, Nick, ol' boy, but we have to catch that buggy."

The desert floor was flat in this area, and the sagebrush and cactus sparse, and Nick liked to run, anyway. They covered ground quickly.

Braddock didn't have to get behind the buggy and chase it, though he was pretty sure Nick could have overtaken it. Instead, he was able to head at an angle to intercept the buggy.

He had made half the distance to the racing buggy when he could see that it was indeed Sally and that she had not lost control but was whipping the horse to a frenzy, tearing along the road and spewing dust in a high cloud behind her.

He gave Nick a couple of more kicks, and the horse surged, his great legs reaching and pumping, enjoying the race with the vehicle. They were running almost parallel now, two dust clouds tearing along the desert, getting always closer.

Then, as Sally glimpsed the rider racing to catch her, she pulled back hard on the reins. It took a while for the horse and buggy to stop, and once stopped, the well-lathered buggy horse kept prancing, its flanks heaving as it sucked in gulps of air.

Braddock pulled up Nick next to the buggy. Nick was pretty well worked up too, but he had not had the run of the buggy horse. Still, Nick kept turning in circles, and Braddock had to keep looking over his shoulder to see Sally.

"You want to kill that horse, Sally?" Braddock asked, not angrily, because he was sure Sally knew what she was doing.

Sally stood up in the buggy. "Clay! They're going to hang Doug McIntyre!"

"What? Who? Where?"

"That gunfighter Hanson and some of his men, and Sperry and some of the other Davis hands. I was coming to get you. I hoped you'd gone back to town."

"So that's what Davis and Harlan were referring to. They knew what Hanson was up to even when we were talking to them at the ranch. Probably figured there'd be no need to talk to McIntyre by tonight. But how do you know this? Where'd you see them?''

"I came across them soon after it happened. They ambushed Doug and some of his hands right on this road.''

"Of course. McIntyre mentioned yesterday he was sending them into town today.''

"At least one man was killed,'' Sally continued. "I saw his body. They took the rest of them prisoner, but they said they were going to hang Doug as soon as they found a tree.''

"Finding a tree might not be easy in this country. Do you think they're taking Doug back to the Davis ranch?''

"No.'' She shifted to the far side of the buggy and pointed from underneath the canopy. "You see that knob in the distance, the yellow one with the brown streak through it?''

Braddock squinted and looked. The shimmering heat waves blurred objects in the distance, but he thought he spotted the landmark she was referring to. "Yes, I see it.''

"There's a dry creekbed just beyond it. Some trees used to grow by the creek. They're dead now but still standing. That's the direction they headed. You'll have to hurry. They're probably already there.''

Braddock nodded. "You have to get to town. Harlan, Randy, and I were ambushed by Milo and his men. Harlan's hurt and needs your help.''

Sally put her hands to her head and moaned. "That

can only make things worse yet. Clay, how can men keep doing the exact opposite of what's needed to prevent more bloodshed?''

"Good question. And we also found Willard Pyle's body. Whoever killed Earl killed him too.''

"But why? Richards said Willard was a partner in the murder.''

"I figure Willard knew it wasn't Doug McIntyre.''

Sally gasped. "But they're going to hang him!''

"I'm going to try to stop it. Hurry to town and get that bullet out of Harlan Davis.''

He gave Nick a good jab with his heels and they were off at a gallop again. As he raced along, Braddock tried hard to think of what he could do once he got there. He might be too late already, but even if he wasn't, he was still just one man, one man with a badge that no one seemed to pay much attention to.

As he raced along the desert, he saw the basin with the yellow streaks where a creek used to be. A few gray skeletons of trees baked in the sun, and at the foot of one of them was a large gathering of horses and men. No one was hanging from a tree yet, but a rope was already over a limb, and Hanson was holding the noose end. Braddock noticed that Hanson was arguing with some of the other men.

With his hands tied behind him, Doug McIntyre was being pushed next to his horse. But nobody seemed to be doing anything beyond that. Then someone noticed Braddock's approach.

The men turned to look at him. Carbines came up.

Hanson stepped forward and lowered one of the carbine barrels. He waved casually toward Braddock as he reined in Nick. " 'Afternoon, Marshal,'' he called calmly.

Braddock leaped from the saddle while a panting, prancing Nick was grabbed by a cowhand. He didn't draw his pistol and he didn't grab his Winchester. Faced with so many men, he knew that that would have been useless. He would have to talk them to a stop.

McIntyre looked terrified but proudly defiant. There were four of his men, including Ned Early, standing nearby in a cluster, disarmed and guarded by Jim Wells, Dave Reever, and two other gunfighters whom Braddock remembered from the saloon. Lowell Sperry was there with five or six other Davis cowhands.

"You can't hang this man!" Braddock roared.

Hanson patted him on the shoulder. "Hey, take it easy, Braddock. We're just doing your job for you."

Sperry said, "He killed Earl, and we're going to hang him for it."

"This is murder," Braddock reminded him. "This man has a right to a trial."

"We did that already," Hanson said. "Now we're going to execute him." He slapped the noose on the palm of his hand.

Sperry put his fists on his hips. "He's guilty, Marshal."

There was a scuffle in the background. Ned Early was struggling with his captors. "No, he's not!" he screamed. "We've been trying to tell 'em that, Marshal."

Dave Reever whipped Early across the face with a pistol barrel. "Shut up!"

Early fell to his knees. He shook his head and looked up at Braddock. "Marshal, I was with Doug when Earl was killed. A lot of us were. He couldn't have done it." Then he got a boot in his face, and he toppled over backward.

Braddock glared at Sperry. "I don't think he did it, either." He pointed to Early on the ground. "What makes you think he's lying?"

"He's McIntyre's top hand," Sperry said.

"Would you lie for Davis?"

"Yeah, probably."

"If a man's life depended on it?" Braddock asked, pointing at McIntyre. "And a lot more men's lives, to boot. Just what do you think Doug's father's going to do when he hears about this?"

"Jud Davis is a father too," Sperry said. "All he's doing is making Doug McIntyre pay for killing his son."

"But how do you know it was Doug?"

Sperry snorted. "Mr. Richards saw him."

Braddock noticed Doug McIntyre's hat trampled on the ground. He scooped it up and shoved it under Sperry's nose. "All Richards saw was a hat that looks like this."

"Good enough for me," Sperry said. "There isn't another one in the valley that looks like that."

"Don't you think anybody could make one that looks like this from a distance?" Braddock asked angrily. "Just put two conchos on any old brown hat."

"We're wasting time," Hanson said. "Come on, boys. Get him up on his horse there." With a quick flip of the rope, the noose was around Doug's neck and quickly tightened. Hanson stood back while a cowhand and a gunfighter grabbed Doug and started to hoist him into the saddle. But Doug resisted, and he was a powerful man. Hanson lent a hand and so did several others.

Braddock stuck a thumb under his vest and pushed his badge forward for Sperry's inspection. "Look," he said. "Anybody could just cut the bottoms off two tin cans and stick them on a hat. Richards wouldn't know the difference from the distance he was at. Did you see the spot? Were you there?"

"I was there," Sperry said. "I saw Earl's body. I saw the bullet holes. And Earl was a good man."

Braddock clenched his hands in exasperation. "We're not talking about that! We're talking about who killed him!"

Doug McIntyre was sitting resignedly in the saddle now. Hanson was tying the end of the rope to the tree trunk, and the noose was tight against Doug's neck and cheek. "It's no good, Marshal," Doug said. "But thanks for trying."

Braddock yelled, "No, not this way!" He drew his pistol, but he didn't even get it leveled before Jim Wells bashed him on the head with the butt of his pistol. As

Braddock sagged, he was manhandled from behind by Wells and another gunfighter. The pistol was twisted from his hand, and his arms were pinned behind him.

Hanson motioned to the horse's rump. "Sperry, you want the pleasure of sending Earl's killer to his reward?"

Sperry shook his head slightly. "No, you can do it."

Braddock shook his head to clear it. He tried to free his arms, but the men holding him were strong. "Don't do it! It wasn't Doug. Sperry, why was Willard Pyle killed?"

Sperry turned his head. "Willard killed? How do you know that? He disappeared."

"We found his body near where Earl was shot. Doug McIntyre would have had no reason to kill Willard. They were working together. It must have been someone else. Don't you see?"

"Doug just didn't want any witnesses."

"Then why let Richards get away? Don't you think that Doug and Willard could have stopped Richards if they had wanted to?"

Sperry squinted at Braddock.

"They wanted you to think it was Doug. They had to let Richards get away."

Sperry turned to look up at Doug McIntyre on the horse. "Hanson," he said, and raised a hand slowly. Hanson took off his hat and gave a yell.

"Wait!" Sperry called.

Hanson swatted Doug's horse on the rump. The horse leaped forward.

A man being hanged from a horse doesn't get a sudden drop and a quick end. Instead, he usually just strangles in agony, swinging and twisting in thin air, feet kicking. Doug gave one jerk of his legs as his horse moved from underneath him, and he swung back at the end of the rope.

But Hanson had not chosen well. As soon as Doug got to the end of the first swing, the full weight of his big frame snapped the tree limb. Doug landed on his knees in the desert sand and then flopped flat on his face. The rope and limb landed on top of him.

Some of the men gasped. Hanson swore, and then he yelled at the top of his lungs, "Get him up! Get him up! Over to the other tree! Get his horse!"

None of Davis's men moved, though. They were stunned by the turn of events. Hanson motioned to two of the gunfighters, and they grabbed Doug and hauled him to his feet.

Braddock glared at the foreman. "You've got a second chance, Sperry," he said. "Let me take McIntyre to jail. Let's have a trial, a real trial."

Hanson had moved Doug to another dead tree and was throwing the rope over a limb.

Sperry snorted. "With twelve of McIntyre's men on the jury."

"No, with men from someplace else. Have the trial someplace else. Think, Sperry! What if Doug didn't do it? Not only will you be hanging an innocent man, but the real killer will still be loose.''

Hanson was helping Dave Reever and another gun-fighter hoist Doug into the saddle of his horse again. Sperry took a step forward. ''Hold it, Hanson,'' he said.

Everyone froze. Hanson looked back at Sperry. ''What for?''

''This is spooky,'' Sperry told him.

Braddock noticed that several of the cowhands were nodding vigorously.

''I'm just not sure anymore. I'm giving McIntyre to the marshal as his prisoner for trial.'' Sperry turned to Wells and the other gunman holding Braddock. ''Let him go.''

Neither man let go. Wells snapped, ''We don't take orders from you. If Hanson says—''

A cowhand jammed a pistol hard into the small of Wells's back. ''Well, *we* take orders from Sperry,'' he said. ''And when the foreman says to let the marshal go, you let him go.''

Braddock was released. He sighed and stretched his back muscles and massaged his neck and the bump on his head. ''Sperry, you won't regret this.''

''I don't know. Mr. Davis might not be happy about this.''

Braddock glanced at Hanson. Hanson was furious, and he looked determined to hang Doug no matter what Sperry said.

"You're right, Sperry," Hanson said. "Mr. Davis is not going to be happy about your stopping this."

"He doesn't own me. Now hand Doug over to the marshal here."

Hanson paused. He could see that all of the Davis cowhands had brought up carbines or drawn pistols. The gunfighters looked at him for direction. Braddock was not sure what to expect. In a shoot-out, Hanson and his seasoned gunfighters would still have the edge, even though outnumbered. But he hoped that Hanson wouldn't see any point to a shoot-out just to hang Doug McIntyre. The man meant nothing to Hanson personally. It was just a job.

Braddock was right, and he sighed in relief when Hanson merely shrugged and said, "Okay, you explain to Mr. Davis what you're doing."

Sperry walked over to Ned Early and the other McIntyre hands. "Go tell McIntyre what happened. His son's in jail, but he shouldn't try to bust him out or we'll hang him."

Early and the other three men nodded. "You done right, Sperry," Early said. Sperry didn't react, and the McIntyre men headed quickly for their horses.

Braddock picked up his pistol, holstered it, and then stepped to Sperry's side. Sperry said to him, "I ain't sayin' you're right, but I ain't sayin' you're wrong, either." He took a deep breath and let it out slowly, looking away. "You know," he resumed, "Hanson killed one of Doug's men back on the McIntyre road when we took him."

"Yes, Sally Anderson told me."

"Understand this—he took a shot at us, so it was fair. But I'll be able to sleep better if it turns out that Doug really did kill Earl. So that fellow on the road didn't die for nothin'." Sperry walked away.

Braddock didn't have an answer for that, just a thought that a lot of men had already died uselessly.

Hanson came up, smiled, and gave Braddock a cuff on the shoulder. "Not bad for a cowhand playing marshal."

"You don't sound mad that I managed to stop you."

Still smiling, Hanson wagged a finger in Braddock's face. "Never get angry. A man doesn't think straight when he's angry."

"That would apply to most of the men in this valley right now."

Hanson chuckled. "Probably right about that." He waved a hand toward Doug McIntyre, who was being hoisted into his saddle one more time. His hands were still tied, but this time he didn't have a noose around his neck. "Marshal," Hanson said, "take your prisoner."

Chapter Nine

Braddock turned the big iron key in the cell lock and heard the bolt strike home. He removed the key and looked into the cell at Doug McIntyre sitting on the simple cot.

"You don't really think there'll be a trial, do you?" Doug said with a smirk on his face.

"No. But you weren't so smug a short while ago."

"My father will be coming into town right away to get me out."

"Him or Jud Davis. Either way, I think you got a slim chance of not being dead soon. You and a lot of other men."

"You know I didn't kill Earl Davis, don't you?"

"But if *you* didn't, who did? At least the bad blood between the Davises and the McIntyres gives some reason, dumb as it is. Who else would want Earl dead?"

Doug shrugged. "He was pretty cocky. A lot of men in the valley didn't like his arrogance."

Same probably goes for you, Braddock thought. "Hardly enough reason to kill a man," he said.

Doug just smiled. Finally he asked, "You going to try to stop my father from getting me out?"

"Nope. I'm in no hurry to die."

"Smart and sensible, Marshal."

"But I'll be honest with you. If Davis shows up first, I won't try to stop him, either. A Davis bullet can kill me just as easily as a McIntyre bullet can."

Doug said nothing, but his smugness faded.

Braddock left the cell area, went into the office, and tossed the key ring on the desk with a clatter. He slumped down into the desk chair and started to swivel.

Both Davis and McIntyre were coming into town for Dr. Anderson's funeral *and* to get Doug out of jail. After the bushwhacking of the Davis boys and the attempted hanging of Doug, Braddock didn't think that either man would feel much like talking, no matter what they had agreed to earlier in the day. And if he tried to stop either rancher, he could wind up looking like that trampled rustler.

The door opened and Sally entered. He sat up straight as she sank into a chair facing the desk. She smiled. "I'm proud of you, Clay. I don't know how you did it, but you stopped the hanging. The whole town knows about it too. My father was right about you."

"Well, I do a lot of dumb things. But this isn't over yet."

Sally's smile evaporated. "I know."

"Did you fix up Harlan Davis?"

"Got the bullet out and bandaged him up. He lost a lot of blood and there was severe pain, but it really wasn't critical. He wouldn't stay in town, though, and went right back out to the ranch.''

"Can't blame him. Milo's probably still hunting for him.''

"What are you going to do now?''

"I know what I would like to do, and that's get on Nick and ride out of here right now.''

Sally slumped back a little. "I'd miss you, Clay.''

"Sally, you're the only thing still keeping me here.''

She frowned, torn by conflict. "I don't want you to stay, because I'm afraid you'll get hurt or killed. But I don't want you to leave, either, because I'll—''

The office door burst open and Richards, Taylor, and Bennett rushed in. They didn't even say hello, but just barged up to the desk and confronted Braddock.

"Are you crazy, Marshal?'' Richards asked.

"Probably,'' Braddock said. "Where I come from, only a crazy man would be doing what I've been doing lately.''

Taylor pounded a fist on the table. "You're right about that!'' He pointed frantically back toward the cell area. "You have to let him go.''

Braddock frowned. "Davis will hang him if I let him out. He's safer in here for the time being.''

"But McIntyre will tear this town apart to get his boy out,'' Richards said.

Braddock nodded. "Guess I'd do the same if I was his father.''

"And if McIntyre doesn't get him out,'' Bennett said, "Davis will tear the town down to get at him.''

"So you want to get Doug out of town and let all the killing happen somewhere else, huh?" Braddock asked.

"It's beyond our control," Taylor told him.

"It's not our fight," Richards said.

"You weren't worried about what would happen to the town while all the gunfighters were just spending their money here," Braddock reminded them.

Now Richards pounded on the desk. "The man's guilty. Why try to protect him? Let Davis have him. You shouldn't have interfered today. It'd be over by now."

"What they were doing was wrong, whether Doug's guilty or not," Braddock said. "But that's not why I tried to stop it. Have you ever seen a real range war before? If Doug had been hanged, it wouldn't have been the end but the beginning."

"Bah!" Richards spun about and stalked a few paces aside.

"Besides, I don't think Doug did kill Earl. You didn't see the look on Ned Early's face when he was begging me to stop Doug from being hanged. I don't think he was lying about being with Doug when Earl was killed."

Taylor pointed at Richards' back. "But Richards saw him!"

Braddock took off his hat and plopped it onto the desk. "All Richards saw was a hat. And why would McIntyre kill Willard Pyle?"

Richards turned around. "Willard? The Davis cow-hand?" He stepped closer. "What do you mean?"

"The Davis boys and I found Willard's body. He was killed at the same time Earl was. But not at the same spot. He was chased down and killed. The killer didn't want a witness."

"What's so strange about that?" Taylor asked. "If *you* murdered a man, would *you* want witnesses?"

Braddock pointed at Richards. "But the killer let Richards go, because he knew Richards would claim it was Doug who did it. Willard could have said otherwise."

Bennett looked at Richards. "Did Willard shoot at you too?"

"I don't know," Richards said. "Earl was the one who had a gun. I took off as soon as the shooting started, and I didn't look back, believe you me."

Taylor asked, "Who else but a McIntyre would want to kill Earl Davis, anyway?"

"I don't know," Braddock said. "I was hoping you could come up with some quick ideas."

Richards threw up his hands. "It doesn't matter, gentlemen. Davis doesn't care. He wants Douglas McIntyre dead, and he's going to get his way whether we like it or not, no matter what any of us believe."

Bennett nodded. "It's true, it's true."

Sally shook a finger at them angrily. "How can you men even think of letting Douglas hang when you feel he might be innocent? Why don't you stand up to Davis?"

The three men looked aghast.

"Marshal Braddock makes sense to me!" Sally cried.

Richards puffed up his chest. "I'm sorry. Marshal, you either have to let Douglas McIntyre go or move him out of town. That's our decision." Taylor and Bennett nodded glumly.

"I'm not going to do that," Braddock told him.

"But you have to," Richards said. "We *order* you to."

"And if I don't?" Braddock asked. "You going to fire me? Davis and McIntyre and all their men are coming into town in a little while. Who's going to protect your precious town for you? You?"

Sally pointed out: "My father's funeral will be held shortly. Reverend Merriman has arrived. Both Davis and McIntyre promised they would attend. So they're coming into town whether Douglas is here or not."

The three men looked confused, annoyed, dismayed.

"Good day, gentlemen," Braddock said, and motioned them outside. "If you can think of anything to say to Davis and McIntyre to calm them down, I suggest you go say it."

They left, grumbling and frightened.

Sally said to Braddock, "Sounds to me like you intend to stay longer."

He nodded. "I've done a lot of dumb things, and maybe this is the dumbest yet, but it seems that there must be some way of settling this. If only I could come up with Earl's real killer." He looked back at the cell area for a moment. "Of course, I could be completely wrong about all this."

"I don't think you are," Sally said. "You make sense to me."

"Thanks. I'm going to try to convince Davis too. I convinced Sperry enough to get him to stop the hanging, and so maybe I can do the same with his boss. I think it's the only chance of stopping a war to the finish. Sally, how about helping me? We made a pretty good team before. Are you willing to talk to them again? Before the funeral? I don't think they'll wait until after the funeral now."

"Of course," she said.

"And if we can't convince Davis, I'm going to step out of the way and let whatever is going to happen go ahead and happen. Would you think ill of me if I did that?"

Sally slowly shook her head. "In fact, I'd think ill of you if you got yourself killed."

Braddock smiled. "Sally, I've been wanting to ask you—"

The office door burst open. It was Josh Miller. He rushed right up the desk. "There's a lot of people headin' for town. The Davis bunch is comin' in from the west and the McIntyres are comin' in from the east. You can see the dust clouds. Must be fifty on each side, maybe more. Others have already drifted into town."

"Josh, you think you could get a message to both

Davis and McIntyre before they get to town?'' Braddock asked.

''Well, if I hurry, I guess I could.''

''Tell them both that Sally and I want to talk to them before the funeral, just the two of them—together. We want to try to convince Davis that Doug McIntyre is the wrong man, and I want to try to get them to cooperate during this drought and head off a range war. Tell them that Sally's asking it over the grave of her father.''

''They're sort of responsible for his death,'' Miller said angrily.

''It worked earlier, and maybe it'll work again.''

As Miller rushed off, Braddock stood up slowly and walked over to a front window. Sally got up and joined him.

''You're not optimistic, are you?'' she asked.

''No. Are you?''

She smiled weakly and shook her head slowly. She looked out the window too. ''I think this town is going to see a terrible fight in a short time. Mayor Richards and the others are right to worry. The town could be shot to pieces.''

''And a lot of men too.''

She tucked a hand under his arm and leaned her head on his shoulder. ''I admire you for trying so hard. You could leave right now. That's the sensible thing. But you're staying and risking everything.''

Braddock put his hand on hers. She smiled up at

him, and he returned the smile. "You ever been to the Yellowstone in Montana?"

"No." She smiled again. "Are you suggesting I go take a look at it?"

"Well, I've had this powerful thought for a long time, Sally Anderson. Well, not a real long time. Matter of fact, just since yesterday."

"What is that thought, Clay Braddock?"

"Well, I've been thinking about making a real home up on the Yellowstone. I don't mind leaving where I'm from. It's funny, and probably a terrible thing to say or to even think, but my sister's husband dying may have been a help to me. It gives me an opportunity for some real happiness."

"With your sister?" Sally asked.

"No, no, not with a sister, Sally. But with a—well, a—"

"Yes?" She was smiling warmly at him. "With a what?"

A distant gunshot interrupted them. "They're starting already," he said. He looked back out the window. "With so many angry men in a town, it has to explode."

Sally's head pressed into his shoulder again. She snuggled closer. "More men dying. Just like my father. A life cut short by a bullet. Just like my father."

He leaned forward and peered out the window. He couldn't see where the shot had come from. The late-afternoon shadows had crossed the street, but he could see no people about. Suddenly he snapped his head down to look at Sally. "A bullet? Your father was killed by a bullet?"

Sally's head rose sharply. "Have you forgotten already?"

"No, no. I mean, it wasn't a shotgun that killed your father but a bullet? I didn't see your father's body before you and the other women had cleaned it up and prepared it for burial."

Sally's face contorted, and tears started flowing. "Don't you think I can tell the difference between a shotgun blast and the hole from a pistol bullet?"

He kept looking at her intently. "Sally," he said gently, "Wes Carter didn't have a pistol."

He stepped to the desk, picked up the key ring, and handed it to Sally. "Here, take these to your father's office. If either Davis or McIntyre comes directly here, I don't want them to be able to open the cell door easily."

"What are you going to do?"

"First I'm going to check on something at the Desert Hole. Then I'm going to find Davis and McIntyre and bring them to your house."

"Shouldn't I come with you to meet them?"

"We're not at all sure they'll talk," Braddock said. "The lead may start flying as soon as they reach town. And I'll feel better if you are out of the way."

"Always sensible." She leaned up and gave him a quick kiss. "Good luck," she said.

He took her gently by the arms and gave her a longer

kiss. Then he squeezed her arms. "Good luck to all of us. Now get going."

She went around to the back of the jail in order to take a back street home.

Braddock made a hasty trip to the Desert Hole and then returned to the street. There was no one on the south end of the street, but at the north end, in front of the livery stable, a large number of men had gathered, some on horseback and some afoot. He silently praised Miller, who had managed to get the two sides into town without starting a fight.

Braddock could pick out Davis on a horse on the west side, along with his two sons and Lowell Sperry, Jim Wells, Dave Reever, and a large number of gunfighters and cowhands. Taylor and Bennett were standing on the ground and talking up at Davis. But Davis didn't seem to be paying any attention to them.

Hanson was standing on the ground in front of the livery stable and putting a noose in the end of rope he had thrown over the beam of the haymow lift. The eight-by-eight wouldn't break off like the tree limb had.

Across the street from Davis stood McIntyre with Milo, Ned Early, and an equally impressive number of men. Richards was at McIntyre's elbow earnestly gesturing and pleading, but McIntyre didn't seem to be paying him any more attention than Davis was paying to Taylor and Bennett.

Carbines and sidearms were present in abundance on both sides of the street.

Braddock settled his holster on his hip, glanced down

at the tin star on his vest, took a deep breath, and started walking toward the livery stable.

Even though it was early evening, the air was heavy and hot, with not a bit of breeze to help. His steps kicked up dust, and his mouth had gone dry, though the palms of his hands felt sweaty.

Soon the crowd spotted him approaching, and they all stared in his direction.

He saw Josh Miller come forward out of the crowd and stand with his hands in his pockets. Miller didn't look relaxed, and when their eyes finally met, he nervously nodded first to one side and then to the other.

Braddock was amazed that all these men would stand in the open this way. If shooting broke out, there would be the most awful slaughter. Angry men did not think straight.

He reached Miller and stopped. "Is your livery stable the usual hanging place for Green Valley?" he asked.

Miller shook his head vigorously. "No, siree, it sure isn't. I'd be mighty obliged if this whole thing went somewhere else."

Hanson stepped up and nodded politely. " 'Afternoon, Marshal," he said. He was idly flapping the noose against his left palm. "Nice evening for a hanging."

"It depends on whether you expect to be hanged."

Davis shouted from the side, "Braddock, Miller said Miss Sally was going to be with you. She's the only reason I didn't come right to the jail for the murderer."

Braddock turned to face Davis, who was still on his horse well off to the side. "I told Sperry I was going to hold Doug McIntyre for trial."

"Sperry's a good man, and I got the highest respect for him. Best foreman in the valley. And he says he's got doubts about Doug McIntyre's guilt. But I don't."

"And I have no doubts about his innocence," Angus McIntyre said from the other side. "There's nothing to talk about as long as my boy sits in jail. And I, too, want to know where Sally Anderson is. I would have come straight to the jail myself."

"She's sitting by her father's coffin," Braddock said to McIntyre. "With the Reverend Merriman. And I want both you and Jud Davis to come with me and stand around that coffin. Maybe John Anderson's cold body will sober the two of you enough to talk this over before it's too late, before there aren't rows of coffins, with maybe you and your sons and your men in them."

"Talking won't do any good," Davis said. "Earl's dead, and Douglas McIntyre's going to pay for it."

Braddock looked at Davis now. "Doug didn't do it. I'm convinced of that. I want to try to convince you too. And then we can talk about cows and water."

"And if you can't convince me?" Davis asked.

McIntyre shouted, "My boy didn't kill Earl!"

There was a fierceness in McIntyre's eyes that made Braddock sure that no one would hang Doug without killing his father first. And there were an awful lot of Winchesters behind him to make that a costly proposition.

Richards called over to Davis: "Please, just talk. What harm can that do? At least wait until after the doctor's funeral."

"You're just worried about your rotten little town," Davis said. "About your investment, about your bank, and squeezing every penny you can out of us cattlemen."

"I was thinking about lives," Richards protested. "Just look at all of you." His eyes were wide as he gestured with both hands at the crowds of armed men.

Taylor and Bennett also added their entreaties. Davis put a boot to Taylor's chest and sent him sprawling. He turned to Sperry and said something. Sperry lifted his Winchester.

Braddock's hair stood on end, and he shot a glance over at McIntyre. McIntyre had seen Sperry's hostile action, and he snapped an order to Milo. Milo's hand started for his pistol.

Suddenly, Dr. Anderson's shotgun boomed out from behind the crowd. Everyone jumped. Some of the men flopped to the ground, and those who didn't had crouched down instinctively. All the men brought their guns up. A hundred hammers clicked.

Braddock had grabbed the handle of his Colt and turned toward the sound of the shotgun blast. Miller had fallen to the ground with his hands over his head.

Sally shouted, "Listen to me!" She walked into the open yard in front of the livery stable and approached Braddock. She held her father's shotgun with the muzzle pointing skyward. Smoke curled from one of the barrels.

There was a collective sigh of relief. Men got back to their feet or stood up straight.

"Miss Sally," Davis said, "you're going to hurt somebody."

"Listen to me," Sally repeated. For emphasis, she pulled the other trigger, and the blast again made everyone jump. "My father's going to be buried tonight," she said. "You all think he was a good man."

There was a murmur of agreement.

"What did he die for? He would still be alive today if it weren't for this fight between you two ranchers. Now you're about to add to the list of dead. Well, you owe it to my father to talk to Marshal Braddock first. Listen to him. He's a good, sensible man. My father thought so and said he was the only sensible man left in the valley. Listen to him!"

"What's there to talk about?" Davis said angrily. "My son's dead and Douglas McIntyre is going to hang for it."

"No, he's not!" McIntyre shouted.

Sally threw the shotgun down on the ground. "You've never gotten along well," she shouted. "Everyone knows that. That's your nature. But my father always thought that deep down you were both sensible men, fair men who could weigh the consequences of your actions."

Hanson called out: "Mr. Davis, let's get on with it. Are you going to let a woman talk to you like that?"

"This one I will," Davis said quietly.

Sally raised her hands in supplication. "What are you two about to do now? *Why* are you about to do it? I can't understand what's gotten into you. Has this drought robbed you of your brains? You men are like rocks rolling downhill. The longer you roll, the faster you go and the harder it is to stop you. Think!"

The crowd was quiet. Braddock looked at Davis and then at McIntyre. They were both staring at Sally.

She walked toward Davis. "What if it wasn't Douglas, Mr. Davis?" she said. "How are you going to feel if you hang the wrong man, even if you all aren't shot dead trying to do it?"

"It was Douglas!" Davis yelled. "Richards said so."

"Marshal Braddock thinks Richards was wrong."

"What does this pretend-marshal know?" Davis said. "I don't care what he thinks."

"But he's the only one in the valley whose mind isn't clogged by hate and anger—or greed," Sally pointed out. She shot a glance at Richards as she spoke the last word. Then she turned to Davis again. Standing beside his horse, she reached up a hand and put it gently on his arm.

"And grief," she said. "No one doubts your loss and your heartache. And your desire to even the score. That's only natural. But make sure you're right first."

Davis stared down at Sally. He glanced over at Braddock, then back at Sally. He wasn't saying anything.

"My boy didn't do it," McIntyre said firmly but

more quietly than before. "Let's listen to what the marshal has to say," he said. "Over John Anderson's body."

Davis was silent for a long moment. "All right," he agreed finally. "Over John Anderson's body."

Sally sighed in relief. "Thank you. I'll meet you at the office." She turned and started walking.

Braddock took in a deep breath and let it out slowly. He looked at Sally as he fell in beside her. "My compliments, Sally. I wasn't getting anywhere by myself."

She smiled feebly. "Well, you said we made a good team. But now it's up to you. Davis only agreed to listen. Now you have to convince him Douglas didn't kill his son."

The crowd marched up the street toward the doctor's office. Braddock, Sally, and Miller led the way. McIntyre and his men went next, followed by Davis and *his* men. Richards, Taylor, and Bennett huddled together in frantic conference.

"You three should be there too," Braddock called back to them.

"All right, Marshal," they chorused.

The crowds reached the doctor's office. The Reverend Merriman stood up in amazement as the parade of people surged inside. He was clutching a Bible with one hand. "What's the meaning of this?" he asked indignantly.

"We're having a sort of prayer meeting for peace in John Anderson's honor," Braddock told him as he went past him into the operating room.

The operating room was not very large, and more people squeezed in than Braddock had wanted. They gathered around the coffin, still lying on the operating table. Braddock stood at the head, with Sally close by his side and Miller behind her. Davis with Harlan, Randy, Sperry, and Hanson stood on one side of the coffin. They faced McIntyre, Ned Early, Milo, and two McIntyre cowhands on the other side. Richards, Taylor, and Bennett stood at the foot of the coffin. The small room was stifling hot, but Braddock thought that the three town fathers were sweating the most.

"Okay, Braddock," Davis said. "Convince me."

"The only evidence that Doug killed your son is Richards' claim that he saw Doug's hat."

"I *did* see it!" Richards protested.

"No," Braddock said. "There was no hat."

"What?" Davis blurted. Everyone turned to stare at Braddock.

"No hat," Braddock repeated. "And no shell casings and no bushwhacker."

"No bushwhacker?" McIntyre asked. "You mean this Willard Pyle did it by himself? But Richards—"

"Williard didn't do it," Braddock said. "He was chased and shot down by Earl's killer to keep him quiet."

Richards took a step forward and pressed up against the coffin. "Marshal, are you calling me a liar?"

"A liar *and* a killer," Braddock said.

"What!" Now everyone's head snapped the other way to stare at Richards.

"You killed Earl," Braddock said. "I haven't figured this all out yet, but you killed him. And you shot Dr. Anderson too."

A burst of loud exclamations met that statement.

Sally grabbed Braddock's arm. "Clay, I can't believe what you're saying."

"Dr. Anderson was killed with a pistol bullet. But Wes Carter didn't have a pistol, only a shotgun. His own pistol is still at the Desert Hole where I left it with the bartender. I just checked on that. And if Wes had gotten a different pistol, he wouldn't have lost it. He was a professional gunfighter. He would have kept a pistol no matter what."

"But why would Richards shoot the doc?" Davis asked.

"After his arm was amputated, Wes was in a fever and delirious. He must have told the doctor that it was Richards, not Doug McIntyre, who was the one who had shot Earl. The doctor did talk to Richards, and he told Richards what Wes had told him. Probably couldn't believe it. But Richards killed Anderson to make sure he didn't tell anyone else, and then he came up here to the office to try to shoot Wes to shut him up too. That's why the inner room was such a mess when Sally got here."

"It did look like there'd been a fight in here," Sally said thoughtfully. "But Wes was sick and had only one arm. Could he really have fought off Richards?"

"Wes was a tough man and also very desperate. Every man's life is precious to himself. So he fought off Richards and then tried to get out of town by stealing a horse from Miller.''

''Custer's mustard!'' Miller exclaimed. ''So Wes really was trying to kill Richards at the stable. We thought he meant to shoot you but couldn't see straight.''

''Yes. And, Richards, you made sure Wes didn't get a chance to talk to me,'' Braddock went on. ''That's why you opened fire early.''

''This is ridiculous!'' Richards sputtered.

Davis said quietly, squinting at the marshal, ''How would Wes have known that Richards had shot Earl? Wes worked for McIntyre, and he didn't even get here until after Earl had been killed.''

Braddock shook his head slowly. ''Wes was working for Richards.'' He pointed to Richards. ''And those two bushwhackers who tried to kill me on the McIntyre road were sent by you, not McIntyre.''

''What bushwhackers?'' McIntyre asked.

''Elmo said they were supposed to kill the marshal. But McIntyre hadn't known I was the marshal until I talked to him. He wouldn't have had a chance to give those kinds of orders to the two gunmen. But Richards did, and he wanted me killed because he'd already shot the doctor and didn't want me to go after his killer.''

''This is all crazy!'' Richards protested. He started inching to the door. ''Crazy! You're not a real marshal, Braddock! Just a stupid cowhand!''

''You worm!'' Davis roared at Richards. ''You always looked down your nose at us cattlemen. You enjoyed seeing me beg for money, you wanted me to lose the bank shares, to lose everything I spent a lifetime to achieve.''

''Me?'' Richards sputtered. ''You're the one who did the humiliating, treating the town like we were some necessary evil, like a privy out back or something.''

''You really did it,'' McIntyre said. ''You killed Earl. You never did like any of our boys.''

''Earl was the worst,'' Richards snarled. ''Thinking he was better than any of us just because his old man owned a lot of land. Well, you won't own it much longer, Jud Davis.''

McIntyre said angrily, ''You've been deliberately trying to set off a range war. You encouraged all these gunfighters to come into town, knowing they'd stir up trouble. We were already down on our knees from three years of drought. One last push and the bank would foreclose on the mortgages and you'd own the whole valley. That was it, wasn't it? You're a vulture, Richards, a greedy buzzard feeding on the misery of the cattlemen.''

Taylor's mouth was agape. ''I can't believe this, Lester,'' he said to Richards.

Bennett looked around the room, worried. ''We weren't part of any of this!'' he cried. ''Honest.''

Davis pushed Sperry back with a hand so he could move closer to Richards. ''It makes sense,'' Davis said. ''You did kill Earl.''

Braddock had a sudden awful thought. ''Wait a minute,'' he said. ''If Wes and Billy and Elmo were working for Richards and not for McIntyre, then—'' He pointed a finger at Milo.

Richards reached into his vest pocket and whipped out a small derringer. ''Milo! Hanson!''

The two gunmen drew their pistols and pushed away the men standing next to them. McIntyre tumbled to the floor. Sally screamed. As Braddock went for his gun, Milo turned on him and fired. But Braddock swerved and took Sally down with him when he dropped for the floor.

Pandemonium erupted. Sperry leaped on Hanson, but Hanson clubbed him with the pistol. Davis lunged for Richards, and Richards fired his derringer. Davis staggered back. He grimaced but didn't fall.

Milo aimed his pistol at Davis, but Harlan lunged across the coffin and grabbed it. It fired and tore a gash in Randy's arm.

Ned Early drew his pistol and fired it point-blank at Milo. The big man lurched, but he hardly hesitated before jerking the pistol out of Harlan's grasp and putting a bullet into Early's chest. Early smashed up against the wall and fell to the floor. As Milo headed for the door, he crashed into Taylor and sent him sprawling into Bennett. They both went down.

Ignoring his wounded arm, Randy leaped on Hanson. Braddock got to his feet again and brought his pistol up to bear on Hanson, but he couldn't get a clear shot. He started around the coffin.

Hanson shoved Randy back into Braddock, and they

both staggered into the shelves along one wall. Men and shelves crashed to the floor. Hanson was out the door before Braddock could unscramble himself.

Richards had bolted for the door too. He was met by a flood of men rushing into the building at the sound of the shooting.

"What's going on?" the Reverend Merriman shouted, bewildered.

"They shot each other! They shot each other!" Richards yelled.

"Jim, Dave," Hanson called as he burst out through the outside door of the office. His two men joined him as he, Milo, and Richards pushed and shoved their way through the crowd into the open street.

Braddock had to fight with Harlan and Sperry for the door. All three of them charged through the crowd of men and got outside.

"Stop!" Braddock called.

Richards kept running, and Milo shuffled after him. But Hanson, Jim Wells, and Dave Reever slid to a stop, turned around, and opened fire. Braddock and Harlan and Sperry returned the fire.

It lasted only a few seconds. One of Hanson's bullets caught Sperry in the side. Sperry fired another round into the dirt and then sank to his knees. He brought his pistol up again slowly, cocked it, and fired a slug into Dave Reever's chest. The gunfighter sprawled in the dust.

Harlan took his second bullet for the day in his left arm, and the third one went into his right leg. He collapsed with a yell and rolled on the ground. He had only managed to get off two shots, and both of them had missed.

Braddock fired as fast as he could cock and pull the trigger of his pistol. He thought one bullet might have grazed Hanson, but Jim Wells definitely took a bullet in the stomach. Wells stumbled and then sank to his knees. By the time he got his pistol up again, Braddock's last bullet slammed into his head. Wells fell backward and lay still. Hanson had turned and run away.

Braddock cocked the hammer and pulled the trigger repeatedly, only to get loud clicks from the pistol. Randy finally used a hand to lower Braddock's pistol.

"You're empty, Marshal," he said.

Braddock nodded several times. "Yeah, yeah," he said. Then he realized just how hard his heart was pounding. "Look after your brother."

But Randy was already bending over Harlan, who was still rolling and whimpering in agony. Braddock noticed that Randy, after the initial shock had worn off, more or less ignored the flesh wound in his arm.

Braddock went over to Sperry, who was still on his knees and clutching his side. Sperry groaned. "Think Miss Anderson could get this bullet out of me the same as she did for Harlan?" He made no other sound after that, because he was holding his breath to bear the excruciating pain.

Braddock patted him on the shoulder. "Sure," he said.

"Here, lie down." Braddock helped the man lie down in the dust of the street. Davis cowhands gathered around. "Make him comfortable," Braddock ordered.

He hurried into the doctor's office. Many men were inside still. He noticed that the cowhands from both spreads had disarmed every gunfighter in the place.

Inside the operating room, he found the Reverend Merriman rising from Ned Early's side. "Killed instantly," the preacher said. "Let's look to the living, Marshal."

Braddock agreed to that. He saw Sally examining Davis's wound. "You okay?" he asked her.

She nodded. "I'll have to get this bullet out," she said.

"You?" Davis said, incredulous.

"Yes, her," Braddock told him. "And Sperry took one in the side, Sally. And Harlan needs you again too."

"All right. By the way, I sent some of McIntyre's men with the keys to let Douglas out of jail."

"Good," Braddock said.

"Is Harlan hurt bad, Marshal?" Davis asked.

"He's in a lot of pain, but I think he'll be all right."

"What about Randy?"

"A wound in the arm. Doesn't look too serious."

"I have to get Father's bag," Sally said, and she headed for the outer office.

"That's how Hanson managed to show up the very next day," Davis told Braddock. "Richards already had him on hand."

McIntyre had come around the coffin. "Milo and those three men of his were at my ranch the next day too, Jud," he said.

"That Milo has always been going off on his own stirring up trouble or getting me to start something."

"Hanson too," Davis said.

Braddock nodded. "Richards was telling them to do it."

Davis agreed. "It was Hanson's idea to go after Douglas and hang him before you had a chance to stop it, Angus."

"Looks like we've both been bamboozled," McIntyre said.

Sally returned with the bag. "It was a small caliber, Mr. Davis," she said. "I'll get it out quickly."

Davis clamped a hand on McIntyre's shoulder while Sally fussed with his wound. "I almost hanged your boy, Angus. I'm sorry."

"I would have killed you first, Jud," McIntyre said with a smile.

"And I you," Davis pointed out. He was smiling too.

"Sorry about Ned Early," Braddock said.

"He was a good man," McIntyre answered.

"Mr. Davis, you have to lie down," Sally said. "I can't work on you sitting up."

"Yes, ma'am," Davis replied. "Boys, help me to the floor."

Several of his cowhands grabbed the big man and let him down to the floor.

"Miss Sally," Davis said, "we all owe you a lot. I wouldn't have listened to Braddock by himself. And I would have done an injustice. Maybe, if I'd listened to you sooner, more men would still be alive."

"Aye," McIntyre added. "We were on the brink. Your father would have been proud of you." He lightly patted the coffin.

But Sally was busy. "Lie still, Mr. Davis."

"Yes, ma'am." He winked up at Braddock.

"Richards, Hanson, and Milo got away," Braddock imformed them. "Will your men help me catch them?"

"Of course."

"Mine too," McIntyre said. "And Douglas will want to be in on it. He has a score to settle with Hanson."

Braddock was ejecting the empty cartridges from his Colt. "All right. Guess he's got a right."

"Take Richards alive," Davis said. "I want to see him hang."

McIntyre confronted Taylor and Bennett, who were both standing frozen against the wall, faces pale, hands trembling. "I would like a word with you, gentlemen."

Taylor and Bennett both jabbered at once, professing complete innocence of the whole scheme.

Braddock went outside. Sperry and Harlan were still lying on the ground with men kneeling around them. Cowhands gathered around Braddock.

"Marshal," one cowhand said, "we told them gunfighters they'd be better off in Denver. They've all headed for their horses."

Braddock nodded. "Good riddance. Now we need to find Richards, Hanson, and Milo. Take them alive, if you can. Dead, if you have to. Let's go."

Chapter Ten

Bands of cowhands, Davis's men mixed in with McIntyre's, spread out over the small town of Green Valley. It was now completely dark, and every shadow was suspect. Every man knew that Hanson and Milo were deadly shots without the slightest compunction about killing a man. But the three fugitives had disappeared.

The posse checked the livery stable first, and left four men to guard the horses there, but they knew that there were other horses in town. They checked the saloons, peeked carefully into locked stores, and hunted through homes and unlocked buildings. They inspected every small corral or stable in town, and decided to simply gather up every horse they could find. They brought them to the livery stable. But they had found no sign of Richards, Hanson, or Milo.

Braddock was on the main street. He kept his pistol drawn, since he knew he would have to shoot fast if he met up with either Hanson or Milo.

He was trying to calm himself. *An angry man doesn't think straight,* he kept telling himself. And he was puzzled about where the three had gone. It was not unlikely that they had locked themselves in a building, which meant that the posse might have to check every building in the town. Then he had an inspiration. *Now, where would a banker go just before he's about to leave town?* he asked himself. And he replied, *To the bank.*

Braddock took the back street and approached the bank from the rear. He cocked the hammer of the Colt and tried the back door. It was locked.

He put his ear to the door, but he heard nothing. He went to each of the back windows and tried to peer past the shades, but they all blocked the view. He could see no light from inside. There were no side windows.

He stepped quietly onto the front boardwalk and tried to peer in through the big front windows past their shades. But those shades, too, blocked his view. He went to the front double doors and tried both of them. Locked. He put his ear to the door and listened. Nothing.

He clumped noisily off the boardwalk, waited a minute, and then tiptoed back onto the boardwalk and softly approached the front doors again. He put his ear to the door and froze, breathing softly and evenly, trying to catch the slightest sound.

Finally he heard someone say, "Okay, he's gone."

"Shh! Not so loud," came the answer.

Braddock recognized the voices of Hanson and Richards. He heard footsteps and then muffled clinking and rummaging.

He took one step back. He raised a foot and gave

the door a savage kick near the lock. The large glass pane shattered. And the door flew open and banged against the inside wall.

Braddock fired a shot into the interior and rushed in and to the side. He saw a muzzle flash, and a bullet tore a chunk out of the doorjamb behind him. He ducked behind a desk.

"So you were still out there, Braddock," Hanson said. "I should have known you'd be tricky."

"Give it up," Braddock replied. "Those shots will bring every cowhand in town here."

"Rather be killed by a bullet than hang. But I don't intend to die just yet."

Braddock heard mutterings ahead of him in the dark interior.

"What do you care?" Hanson said to Richards. "You're not going to be here anymore, anyway."

Braddock was puzzled by the remark until he heard a match hiss into flame. The room was lit by a flickering light. And then a bright lamp came sailing through the air. It shattered against the side wall six feet from him. The spilling kerosene burst into flames. Braddock felt the heat from the flames just a few feet away. The room was now bathed in harsh, flickering yellow light, and filling with black smoke.

"Time for you to leave, Braddock," Hanson said. He laughed. "Too bad," he added. "I liked you. But a job's a job."

"Hanson, we have to get out of here too!" Richards cried frantically. "Now!"

Braddock heard Hanson push Richards to the floor. "Leave when you want, but the money stays with me, and I want Braddock before I go."

The hot kerosene ran easily, and puddles of burning fluid started creeping under the desk that Braddock was hiding behind. Hanson fired a bullet into the desk. It missed Braddock, but it emphasized his precarious position. The fire had leaped up the wall and was now licking at the ceiling.

He heard Richards snarl, "I want that money!"

"I don't need you anymore!" Hanson snapped back.

Braddock heard them scuffling. With Hanson distracted, Braddock leaped to his feet and hurled himself through the large window in front. The glass shattered into a thousand pieces with a tremendous crash. He rolled on the boardwalk and crunched on the splinters. Hanson sent two bullets after him.

"You let him get away!" Hanson snarled at Richards.

Braddock got to his feet. He figured surprise would be his best weapon, and so he leaped right back into the burning building through the broken window.

He was right. Hanson and Richards were heading for the rear of the bank with their backs toward him. "Hold it!" Braddock shouted.

Startled, Hanson spun around with his pistol up and fired too fast. The bullet tugged at Braddock's sleeve.

Braddock fired at the same time. The slug sent Hanson crashing into the wall. He dropped the bag of money. Hanson brought up his pistol slowly, but Braddock fired again. The second bullet crumpled Hanson to the floor. He landed on top of the money bag.

Braddock heard Richards cursing and fiddling with the lock to the rear door of the bank. He jumped up and headed for the back of the bank.

Richards threw the door open. It banged up against the inside wall. He ran right into Doug McIntyre and Randy Davis.

" 'Evening, Mr. Richards," Doug said.

"We have some unfinished business with you," Randy added.

Richards spun around and tried to run back into the bank, but Doug and Randy grabbed him and jerked him back. Braddock reached the rear door just then.

"Marshal!" Richards shouted at him. "Arrest me. I'm your prisoner. I demand a trial."

Doug and Randy dragged him down the two steps to the ground.

"You'll get as speedy a trial as I got," Doug said.

Six men came around the corner. "I see you got Richards," one of them said. "Where's Hanson and Milo? Here, let us take him from you."

Braddock pointed to the burning bank building. "Hanson's in there, beyond help. I haven't seen Milo."

Neither had anyone else.

"Come on, boys," Doug said. He waved toward the street. "Let's take care of this one and look for Milo later."

There was ready assent to that. Richards was manhandled away. "Marshal Braddock!" he called one more time.

As Braddock watched him disappear around the corner of the building, he thought about that bag of money lying on the floor underneath Hanson. No point in having it burned up. After reloading his Colt, he turned to go into the bank.

He was already too late. The tinder-dry bank building was being gutted. The flames had reached the rear door. Braddock could not see even Hanson's body through the flames, much less the bag of money.

Flames were now eating through the back wall of the bank, and the resulting light drove away shadows near the bank. Braddock looked up and noticed that the roof had been penetrated, and the heat was driving a swirling cloud of smoke, sparks, and burning embers into the air. There still was no wind that evening, so the incendiary matter wasn't carried away. A hot, deadly rain was falling on nearby buildings. Their roofs were already smoldering.

Braddock moved away from the bank building. Milo would surely keep to the dark. Braddock kept to the back of the buildings. He went up the row of buildings, hugging their sides, pausing, listening. He could hear the posse sometimes, but they were heading back to the livery stable. And the noose.

As he reached the back of the Desert Hole he heard glass break inside. He stepped to the open back door and peered into the lighted interior. The saloon was empty except for Milo at the bar, smashing bottles with his pistol barrel.

Braddock brought his pistol up and entered. Milo slowly turned when he heard Braddock's footsteps, but he made no hostile movement. He leaned on the bar for support. His pistol dangled in his right hand at his side.

Braddock stopped well back. He kept his pistol leveled on the gunfighter. "Put the gun down, Milo," he said.

Milo was breathing with labor, and he swayed. He clenched his eyes tightly and then opened them again. Slowly he brought his gun hand up, not to level the pistol at Braddock, but to clutch his stomach.

Braddock could see the large red splotch on Milo's shirt.

Milo snorted. "Me, the toughest gunman in the West, shot by a cowhand."

Braddock realized that Ned Early had probably killed his killer before he died himself.

"I'm taking you prisoner, Milo. Drop the gun." He was surprised that the gunfighter could even stand after having a .45 slug fired into him from two feet away.

"Where's Hanson?" Milo asked.

"Dead."

"Richards?"

"About to be dead, unless I get back and save him from a lynching."

Milo nodded. "Hanson's way was better. Did you do it?"

"Yes."

Milo nodded again. "Braddock, you're the first lawman I ever had any respect for. And you're not even a real lawman."

"I am tonight. You have to come with me."

Milo staggered back a step, then caught himself on the bar. He straightened up, but still held on to the bar with his left hand.

"I'll never hang," he said. He removed his left hand from the bar and stood up straight. Painfully he sucked in his breath once, and then let it out slowly. "Okay," he said. "I'm ready." Slowly, with concentrated effort, he started to raise his right hand with its cocked pistol.

"Don't!" Braddock warned.

But the pistol kept coming up. Braddock fired.

Milo twisted and staggered back. His gun hand dropped and banged against the bar. But he didn't fall.

He braced himself against the bar and slowly pivoted. His right hand came around again. Braddock cocked his pistol and fired once more.

There was a blank look on Milo's face when he crashed to the floor.

Braddock stared at the gunfighter on the floor for a moment. He didn't go closer. Finally he holstered his pistol, turned, and left the saloon through the rear door.

He walked briskly toward the livery stable. The night was lit up with the light from burning buildings. Both buildings next to the bank were crackling fiercely as flames engulfed them. The walls of the bank itself had collapsed inward. Looking back, Braddock saw that even the roof of the Desert Hole was burning.

When he got near the livery stable, he saw four cowhands hoisting Richards into the saddle of a horse standing underneath the haymow lift beam. Richards' hands were tied behind his back and he was pleading frantically. Davis was supervising. The wound in his side didn't seem to slow him down much.

Angus McIntyre was just watching from a short distance away. "It was his boy," McIntyre said to Braddock, "so it's his right."

Braddock shook his head. "It's nobody's right but the law's, and then only after a fair trial by judge and jury. I'm still the marshal here. That man's my prisoner. Turn him over to me."

"The devil I will!" Davis roared. "Let's get on with it. Get the noose on him."

A McIntyre cowhand on horseback sidled up next to Richards with the noose. Two men pulled one of the last of Miller's coffins from inside the stable.

"Stop!" Braddock shouted. "That's an order!" Suddenly he saw Sally and Josh Miller at the edge of the crowd. He strode up to her and said, "Sally, you shouldn't be watching this."

"Yes, I should," she said. "You said we're a team. I belong at your side." She grabbed his hand and pulled him back to where Davis and McIntyre were flanking Richards on his horse.

Sally looked at both ranchers and said, "Not only do I agree with Marshal Braddock, but my father would, too, if he were still alive. Can either of you men doubt that?''

"Miss Sally," McIntyre said in a suddenly weak and faltering voice, "you and the marshal are really asking a lot of us."

"If I am, Mr. McIntyre, it's because I know you men came here to establish strong and healthy roots for your children and grandchildren, and how will they ever be able to live in peace and enjoy their heritage without justice and law and order?''

"She's right," Braddock said. "And I think you both know it in your hearts."

Davis and McIntyre turned to look at each other at the same moment. Then they both growled and nodded their heads.

"Okay," McIntyre muttered to Braddock. "I guess there's no harm in postponing the hanging until it's done more legally."

Braddock and Sally gave a deep sigh, and Sally, smiling at the two ranchers, assured them, "You'll never regret that wise decision."

After that, Braddock ordered several of the ranch hands to conduct Richards to a jail cell. He would be joining them in a minute. Then he turned to Sally and asked, "How are your patients?''

"Sperry and Harlan will be fine after a period of rest.''

"Your surgical skills have been a real blessing to everybody." He touched the stitches in his cheek.

Sally smiled. Then she frowned and touched a blotch

on his sleeve. She noticed other blotches. "This is blood. What have you been doing? I can't leave you alone for a minute."

"Maybe you shouldn't," Braddock said, grinning.

Chapter Eleven

As the crowd dispersed, Davis and McIntyre walked up to Sally and Braddock. Davis took off his hat and said, "We can start the funeral right away, Miss Sally. I'll send some men up with a wagon."

"Thank you," she replied. "I'll tell the reverend."

Davis turned to Braddock. "Marshal," he began, "we want—"

Braddock removed and threw away his tin star. "Sorry, but I'm not your marshal anymore."

Davis bent down and picked up the star. After polishing it on his sleeve, he extended it to Braddock. "I'm sure that Angus here believes as I do, that you deserve to keep this."

"Absolutely," McIntyre agreed. "It'll be a symbol of our respect for you and your judgment. The more I think about it, the more I have to admit that you're right about a trial for Richards."

"We know you're leaving," Davis said, "but we'd be honored if you'd wear this till you left, and then maybe take it with you to wherever you're going. If it weren't for you, probably half the men in this town would be dead by now. And Richards would have gotten away with everything.''

Braddock looked at the badge in Davis's hand. ''Well, where I come from, it'd be impolite to turn down something like that.'' He took the tin star. ''Thank you, gentlemen.''

''Thank *you,* sir,'' Davis replied.

''Here,'' Sally said, ''let me put it back on for you.'' She took the badge and deftly pinned it to Braddock's vest.

They all looked at the fire. The entire block with the bank was fiercely ablaze, and several buildings across the street were burning too. Smoke and burning embers and sparks filled the air in a roaring cyclone above the town.

McIntyre said, ''Taylor and Bennett actually asked for our help to put it out. As if we'd lift a finger, even if there was enough water to do any good, which there isn't.''

Davis looked satisfied. ''Now, as I was saying, Braddock, Angus and I have been talking. We think you're right. If we got rid of half the cows still on this range, maybe sixty percent, the rest could be saved in not too bad a shape. And the range itself would survive in better shape too.''

''The problem,'' McIntyre said, ''is how we figure out what's half.''

''How about just rounding them all up and shooting half of them,'' Braddock suggested.

''But how do I know he'll round up all his cows?''

McIntyre asked. "Then I find out later he only got rid of a fourth of his and I've lost half."

"Why don't you each collect all of the other man's cattle," Braddock suggested. "I'll count them on the hoof and count the carcasses when you're done."

Davis and McIntyre looked at each other and slowly nodded. "That's a good idea, Angus," Davis said. "Here's my hand on it." He offered a handshake to the other rancher.

McIntyre took the offer. "Done," he replied.

Davis turned to Sally. "Miss Sally, this fire is spreading very fast. I suggest you go immediately to your house and salvage anything you want to save. I'm afraid your house is going to burn too. We can have your father's funeral a little later. He'd understand."

"Yes, I think you're right," She turned to Davis. "I'd be grateful if you could lend me a wagon for the furniture."

"Of course, Miss Sally."

McIntyre added, "We'll send all the men you need to carry your things out."

"And you can stay out at my ranch as long as you want," Davis added.

McIntyre pointed toward her house. "Embers are hitting it already. We'll get your father out of there right away and head for the cemetery with Reverend Merriman."

"All right."

Davis and McIntyre turned to look at the burning town. Davis pointed to the bank. The flames were dying down. Most of the building had already been consumed. "Suppose that means our mortgages are cinders now, Angus?"

McIntyre laughed. "Along with all the other assets of the bank." Both men laughed. "Say, the town burning and all these cows we have to kill makes me hungry."

Davis frowned. "You want to eat now?"

"Yep," McIntyre said. "Roast beef!"

They both laughed and headed away together.

Miller pointed toward the smoke rising from the roof of his stable. "Seems like I'd better grab what I can too. It ain't much."

"Sorry, Josh," Braddock said.

"Say, Marshal, do you suppose they could use somebody like me up along the Yellowstone?"

Braddock grinned. "I'll bet they could. You're a handy man to have around. Come along."

"What are you going to do, Miss Sally?" Miller asked. "Ain't gonna be any town anymore."

Braddock stepped closer to her. "She's heading for the Yellowstone too."

Miller grinned broadly. "Grant's gravy."

"Josh," Sally prompted, "don't you have some work to do?"

"Oh, yep, sure do," he said. He gave a laugh and sauntered off toward his stable, looking back over his shoulder.

Sally looked at Braddock. "Just what exactly do you mean, sir?" she asked with a smile. "Surely you're not concerned about finding someone to take those stitches out, are you?''

Braddock chuckled. ''No. It's just that where I come from, you don't break up a good team.''

''A team?'' she asked. ''Just a team?''

''Husband and wife,'' Braddock said. ''That's the best team of all. If you'll have me.''

She smiled and reached her arms around his neck. ''Clay, let's get married right now. Tonight.''

''Reverend Merriman is handy,'' Braddock noted.

''And I know this may sound bizarre, but let's get married in front of my father's grave. I know he would have approved, and I would feel like he was there with us.''

''Sounds fine to me,'' Braddock said. ''Back where I come from—''

Miller turned and called from down the street, ''Say, Marshal, just where exactly are you from, anyway?''

Sally laughed.

Braddock turned his head with a smile. ''Doesn't matter where I'm from, Josh. What matters is where I am going to.''

''The Yellowstone?'' Miller asked.

''Nope,'' Braddock said. ''Paradise.''

Braddock and Sally clung to each other in a long embrace, squashing the tin star between them.